10822359

# Valley of the Spun

Jonathon T. Cross

That Spooky Beach LLC

Book Cover by Deividas Jablonskis

ISBN: 979-8-9883520-6-8

Second edition 2026

This book is dedicated to anyone who's ever lost their way and fought like hell to get it back

*"Happiness is not a goal, it is a by-product. Paradoxically, the one sure way not to be happy is deliberately to map out a way of life in which one would please oneself completely and exclusively. After a short time, a very short time, there would be little that one really enjoyed."*

Eleanor Roosevelt

# The Devil

2008

Blood leapt from one fiber of my shirt to the next, trickling down my ribs. The stars were shining, but they were blurry, incomprehensible, stretching ever onward as my eyelids pressed themselves shut.

It was the end. The culmination of my choices. Like the bloody shirt stuck to my chest, the consequences clung to me, suffocating me. It didn't matter how far I'd come, or how high I'd climbed. I had to face the truth.

The devil is real.

He's not a fallen angel hiding in the shadows. He's a monster that lies dormant inside each of us, begging to be fed.

When life fell apart, I nurtured my devil, and in no time, that fatted calf seized control. Every fear and insecurity became amplified; every action tainted. Before I knew it, I was possessed.

I tried to fight. At one point, I thought I had him beat, but that son of a bitch came back.

As the fog of death thickened, I knew I'd lost once and for all, and I couldn't help but think about everything else I was about to lose. At the forefront of my mind was my daughter, Sadie. It's funny, in a terrible sort of way, that the sole driving force behind all this tragedy was the simple pursuit of happiness.

# HAPPINESS

## THREE MONTHS BACK

Sunlight reflected off the artificial lake, planting a halo on Sadie's head. Her cheeks, flushed and trembling, bore the weight of the Arizona sun, but a smile lingered on her face as she chased a flock of ducks.

Fragrant molecules of cut grass, stolen by the breeze, drifted to my nostrils. The scent was a reminder of a simpler time, a time of happiness and autonomy. I wanted Sadie's entire life to be as perfect as that moment, and as vibrant as the lush grass surrounding us.

But grass doesn't grow in the desert.

The healthy green blades owed their livelihood to the shade of non-native pine trees, the breeze rolling off the artificial lake, and the persistent sprinkler heads, which had soaked the better part of Sadie's outfit.

When the ducks took flight, Sadie ran toward me with her arms outstretched, and for a moment, the world shrank to just the two of us. She looked up at me with her sparkling blue eyes and said her favorite words.

"Up, Daddy."

With a swift motion, I lifted Sadie over my head.

She extended her arms and became an airplane, navigating the skies, tilting her body left and right while shouting, "Whoosh!"

We made three passes around the field and one loop around her stroller before she ordered me to land. I swooped low, then spun her in the air before having her touch down on our picnic blanket.

Eva glared at me from the edge of the blanket. "I hate it when you do that."

I feigned a smile as Sadie ran into her mother's arms, wondering if that was how the rest of my life was going to be, monitored and judged.

Every time I looked at Eva, all I could see was her getting pounded by the guy I caught her cheating with. I tried to push the image away—Ryder's freckled back flexing, a swoop of his strawberry blonde hair caught in her throat.

I snapped back to reality.

Eva's eyes were still fixed on me, glaring over Sadie's shoulder as they hugged. It was a rotten look, one our daughter would always be blind to.

Molecules of cut grass still lingered in the air, but they no longer smelled sweet. It was as if Eva had flipped a switch, plunging the world into darkness. As my happiness faded, I recognized the grass' pungent odor for what it was. A distress signal, a warning to the rest of the field—danger was coming.

"Daddy's so silly." Eva nuzzled her head into Sadie's neck. "What if he dropped you?"

"I would never drop her."

"It's hot," she said as she lifted Sadie into her stroller. "We're leaving."

"What time can I pick her up tomorrow?"

Eva cocked her head. "Tomorrow?"

"My birthday... We talked about this last week."

"I don't think so."

"It's the same day every year," I said. "She's coming over for cake."

Eva craned her neck and pulled her blonde hair back as tight as she could. Her spider-like fingers worked diligently, spinning a web of golden strands together. Like everything else in her life, she needed to pull at it.

"Two days in a row?" she asked.

"Yeah."

A chuckle escaped her lips. "Most men don't get to see their kids."

"I don't care what most men get."

"Enough." Eva drove her heel into the grass.

A passerby turned his ear, watching like he was itching to intervene. It was a scenario I'd encountered often during our relationship. Eva would make a scene, but people always kept their eyes on me, wondering what I must've done to this poor woman and her vulnerable child.

I bit the inside of my lip, swallowing the warm blood that leaked into my mouth. "Sadie deserves a father."

"Then go home, Zeke," she said. "Be happy with what you've got."

As if being happy was something people could just do. Happiness felt like the dew on desert grass. It was unnatural; scarce. Visible for a second before it evaporated, leaving no trace of its existence behind.

It wasn't Eva's attitude, or even her abrupt goodbye, that bothered me the most. It was the gnawing uncertainty she left me with. She'd been driving a wedge between me and Sadie since the day I broke up with her. The question was, how long before the rigid bitch snapped?

# Birthday

A candy pearl dropped from the edge of my cake. The buttercream piping had softened since it came out of the fridge. The pearl bounced off a bottle of Jack Daniel's and landed near my laptop, the only source of light in the dim kitchen.

Vanilla cake is bland, and strawberry icing is overrated, but Sadie would've loved both the flavors and, most of all, the colors. She would have adored the frilly designs and dug her hands straight into the confection.

I heard the front door open. Levi was home. His footsteps carried through the hall and stopped at the edge of the kitchen.

"Hey man," he said, peeking his head in. "You good?"

"Fine."

Levi flipped on the lights and surveyed the table. "I take it Sadie won't be joining us?"

"Some detective you are."

"MySpace, huh?" Levi sat down at the table and took control of my laptop, which was opened to a wall of pictures on Ryder's MySpace page. "Why are you doing this to yourself?"

"Eva told me Sadie wasn't feeling good today."

I stole the laptop back and clicked on the photos she'd been posting. Ryder and Sadie were sharing an ice cream in one. In another, he was lifting Sadie over his head—something I wasn't allowed to do.

"At least Sadie is having fun," Levi said.

I slammed the laptop shut. She wasn't just having fun. She was ecstatic, wearing that big, happy, unencumbered smile of hers. "She should be having fun with me, not with Ryder."

Levi shrugged. "Maybe he's just a nice guy."

"He's a douche."

"Eva's the person who cheated on you. Be mad at her."

"I shouldn't have to be mad at anyone." I pounded my fist on the table, sending the decorative pearl airborne. "Life should just work for me the way it works for everyone else."

Levi exhaled slowly.

I grabbed the bottle and downed a swig of whiskey. "Say what you wanna say."

"You've been spiraling since Mom passed." Levi's eyes moved to the crucifix hanging around my neck, a communion present from our mother. "I haven't seen that in a long time."

"It makes me feel better."

"Does it?" Levi asked. "I thought you..." he said, using air quotes, "swore that shit off."

"It just does."

I put a Marlboro Red between my lips, flicked the flint wheel of my Zippo, and inhaled. The cigarette's fiery red ember quickly turned to ash as the noxious smoke invaded my lungs.

Levi snatched the cigarette and knocked the cherry out. "Not in the house."

"I know, I know, it's a rental."

He crumpled the cigarette and flicked it into the trash. "You can't keep doing this."

Having an older brother sucked nuts. He was like an overprotective parent, hovering and judging.

"What do you want from me?" I asked.

"I want you to take charge of your life, dude. If you don't like things, then do something about it. Tell that bitch you're gonna get a lawyer. Stop using MySpace to stalk her boyfriend."

# CHECKMATE

## THE NEXT MORNING

I hated the idea of taking legal action, but I needed a plan, so I wrote up a parenting schedule. Eva wouldn't answer her door when I tried to show it to her, though. I should've walked away, but something in me snapped.

After a few minutes of pounding, my persistence paid off, and the door swung open.

"What?" Eva demanded, her eyes on fire.

I had a whole speech planned, but I choked. The schedule was scrunched in my fist, stained with sweat, and the only thing I could blurt out was the unadulterated truth.

"I deserve time with Sadie."

"It's seven in the morning," she snapped. "Are you serious?"

"This is a parenting schedule," I said, forcing the papers on her. "People get to spend birthdays with their kids, and see them on holidays, and take them to the fucking park alone."

Eva snatched the papers. "You wrote this?"

The condescension dripped from her lips. Yeah, I wrote it... and it was about doing the right thing, not a legal contract, but she wasn't having it.

Ryder walked up behind her, with Sadie passed out in his arms.

"Take *my* daughter to the bedroom," Eva told him. "I have to deal with this."

Ryder turned and walked down the hall. Sadie, half-awake, waved goodbye to me over his shoulder as they disappeared. She had no idea what was going on, and that was a good thing, because Eva activated bitch-mode.

"Here's what I think," she said, tearing the papers in half.

I don't know if it was the whiskey simmering in my gut, or the sleepless night, but when that schedule hit the ground, my heart went into overdrive. It took everything in me not to reach out, grab her bun, and snap her neck.

"You don't get to dangle Sadie over my head."

"Don't you have work?" she asked, checking an imaginary watch.

"Wouldn't it be a shame if I couldn't pay for the daughter I'm not allowed to see?"

Eva doubled down. "Get out of my house."

"I may have written *this* schedule, but a lawyer is gonna draft the next one," I told her, "so have a great fucking day, and the next person at your door is gonna be a process server."

"Excuse me?"

I never should've shown her my hand. And I probably shouldn't have marched through her flower garden either. She chased me through the yard, caught me by the shoulder, and dug her nails in.

"You can't handle being a parent," she said, digging deeper.

I pivoted, twisting her wrist until she let go of me. "I wouldn't know, would I?"

Ryder appeared just in time to see Eva whimper.

She knew what she was doing. It was all maneuvering. Victimhood was her way of life. It's one of the reasons she hated me so much: because she couldn't control me, but she had her hooks in Ryder alright. The queen stepped aside, and he strode outside like a rook sliding clean across the board.

Checkmate.

Ryder's fist caught the side of my skull, twisting my head around. Then he tackled me and shoved my face in the dirt. The taste of blood and soil lingered in my mouth as he pulled my head back and slammed it down again. Things could've gotten uglier, but Eva called her dog off and they hurried back inside. It wasn't about mercy for her, it was self-preservation.

I brushed myself off and blinked the dirt from my eyes, but the grit clung to my clothes. I'd have to show up to work looking like a train wreck, not that it mattered. The job was a soul-suck, and I couldn't bring myself to care about it.

# Valley of the Sun Mortgage

I worked as a subprime mortgage collector, a job that was as simple as it was miserable. Track down people who couldn't afford to pay their bills and pressure them into paying. I was a loan shark, minus the baseball bat.

The auto-dialer placed a call, but I didn't say anything when the guy picked up.

"Who is this?" he asked.

"...Good morning," I said at last. "This is Zeke with—"

I disconnected mid-sentence so it would sound like the line dropped. After all, our calls were recorded for quality assurance.

Debt collection wasn't my first choice, but it was the only job that paid over ten bucks an hour without a degree. Cracks were forming, though. I didn't know where they would lead, but they were spreading fast.

Call volume was up, and payments were down. People were losing their homes. They turned to rentals, making rental demand shoot up. It affected everyone, me and Levi included. Our landlord kept upping the rent, which meant I needed the job more than ever, despite hating every second of it.

When no one was looking, I cracked open my file cabinet drawer and knocked back a whiskey shooter, savoring that sweet burn. Then, I placed the dialer on hold and did a web search for lawyers.

A hundred bucks an hour, two hundred? Get the fuck out. How was anyone able to afford that shit? After some searching, I found a lawyer who offered free consultations and weekend appointments, so I booked for Sunday. Then I left the dialer on hold and excused myself. The smoking patio was calling my name.

As the sunshine warmed my face, I lit a cigarette, trading the morning air for the sweet, smoky scent of tobacco. Another agent, Damien, followed me outside with a smoke hanging out of his mouth.

He patted his pockets, the universal code for help, so I lit him up.

"You're a goddamn lifesaver, brother." Damien blew a cloud of smoke into the air. "You good? Lookin kinda pale 'n shit."

"That's just how white people look," I joked.

Damien chuckled. "Saw you got reamed by Davie for being late."

Davie was the big boss. The type of asshole who starts a 'Fun Committee' to distract people from the fact that they're being systematically drained of their life's passion. And the guy had it out for me too. I didn't really feel like talking about Davie, so I just nodded and smiled.

Damien took another puff, intent on keeping the conversation going. "Calls have been something."

I turned away, trying to hide my black eye. "Yep."

"Ain't nobody sayin it," he added. "But you know it's a recession."

"Yeah." I exhaled a cloud of smoke. "Things are getting bad."

"You good, man... like, for real though?" Damien eyed me like he knew the comment was about more than the financial market.

"Why do you ask?"

Damien pointed at my face. "'Cause you got your ass beat, homie."

I drew a long breath of my cigarette, holding the smoke in as the toxic fumes impaired my senses. I don't know why it bothered me to hear him say that, but I didn't want everyone to know that my world was falling apart.

"We can't all be six-foot-five linebackers," I said.

Damien flicked his cashed cigarette into the street. "You still got my number?"

"Yeah, why?"

"You're gonna come hang with me this weekend, let loose."

"Thanks, but I'm busy."

I needed to detox, save money, and prepare for my consultation. Thirty minutes of free advice, that was it. Then I'd have to take on Eva by myself or shell out thousands of dollars I didn't have.

"I throw sick parties," Damien said as he headed back to the office. "You should think about it."

# The Consultation

Soap dripped off the panels of my sun-faded '88 Toyota Corolla, revealing the cracked white paint beneath. I tossed the squeegee, wiped my hands, and admired my ride. Cleanliness is godliness; that's what Mom always said.

The car was a beater, with a taped-on mirror and messed-up trim, but I loved her. I even named her Dethbox after my favorite band, Megadeth. She was almost as old as me, and she'd seen some shit.

Like me, she was rough around the edges, but she gave it her all, and she deserved to look her best. And when I met with the lawyer for my consultation, I was going to present the best version of myself too.

Levi leaned out the front door. "Dude, you gotta go."

"On my way."

I hopped into the Dethbox, stepped on the clutch, and pumped the gas. Then I turned the key. The dashboard lights flickered out. I rubbed the dash for good luck, pumped the gas and tried again, but the engine just sputtered.

There was one pump left in her before the engine flooded. I turned the key and prayed. The engine sputtered and popped, then with a reluctant gurgle, it chugged to life. Gasoline fumes filled the interior, mixing with the stale upholstery as the air conditioner blew piping hot air at my face.

My phone buzzed right before I left.

It was Eva. Her voice was almost lost to the engine. "How's your face?"

"My what?"

"Your face," she repeated.

I checked my bruise in the mirror. "How do you think?"

"Sadie misses you."

"Why are you telling me this?" In all the years I'd known Eva, she'd never come that close to apologizing for anything.

"Do you miss her or not?" she asked.

"Yeah."

"We're out shopping... Meet us at K-mart?"

Eva was perched on the hood of her Lexus, phone pressed to her ear, as I pulled into the K-mart lot. I parked right behind her. Sadie, always observant for a little kid, popped her head up from her rear-facing car seat. The second she heard the screech of the Dethbox's brakes, she knew her dad was there.

She struggled against her car seat. Then, growing frustrated with the straps, threw her rattle at the rear window, leaving a trail of viscous slobber dripping down the tempered glass.

As I reached for her door, a black SUV came tearing down the aisle and skidded to a stop in front of the Lexus. Eva jumped off the hood and cowered behind the SUV. Then the driver stepped out. He was a big motherfucker, at least twice my size. Something was about to go terribly wrong.

"Ezekiel Graves," he said.

I cocked my head. "Who the fuck are you?"

The guy shoved a manila folder into my chest. "Doesn't matter who the fuck I am. Get back in your car and read these papers."

"Are you serious?" I asked.

"Get back in your car." The man repeated. "Go home and read that shit real good."

I don't know what I was thinking. All I knew was that Sadie was right there in front of me, and I couldn't let anyone take her away—I opened the Lexus's back door.

Before I knew it, the guy had grabbed me and smashed my face into the back window. My bloody spit dripped down the glass, parallel to Sadie's drool. Her sweet smile had faded, and her face was full of tears. She didn't know what was happening.

I smiled at her one last time, so she'd remember me happy, even if it was a lie.

# Order of Protection

The bartender measured two shots of Jack into a rocks glass, topped it with a splash of Coke, and dropped a cocktail straw in before sliding the drink over.

I snatched the glass off the bar top and held it to my mouth, allowing the fizz to pepper my nostrils. My body shuddered at the scent, priming itself.

"Leave it open," I said, tossing him my card.

The whiskey lit a trail down my esophagus, igniting like a fireball when it reached my stomach. I know, drinking isn't the answer, but I didn't know what else to do. I brought my drink to the patio and found an empty table in the corner.

The order of protection I'd been served earlier was folded up in my pocket. I reread it, hoping the words would've changed somehow.

**"Zeke showed up at my house uninvited..."**

Every lie starts with a kernel of truth. But when you're never invited to the house where your daughter lives, uninvited is the only way to show up. Reading the facts didn't bother me. It was Eva's lies that pissed me off.

**"...He attacked me..."**

I dragged my hand down my face, rereading her bullshit.

**"...He injured my daughter in the struggle... We're afraid for our safety."**

How dare she write "we" as if Sadie shared in her delusions. Sadie wasn't even awake, let alone present. There was so much rage building inside me, and there was nothing I could do with it. If I so much as texted Eva, then per the order, I could get thrown in jail.

While I was busy dwelling on all the stuff I couldn't change and all the things I couldn't do, Levi strolled out the patio door and pulled a chair next to me.

"So, here you are," he said, looking at my drink.

"How is this possible?" I asked as I raised the glass to my lips. "Eva made up lies, with no evidence, and got an order of protection barring me from my daughter for an entire year."

"It's only a year, at least," Levi said.

He had no understanding of children, or how quickly they can forget. Sadie was going to have so many firsts that I'd miss, and form strong bonds with everyone but me, and I could never recreate those.

"Sadie won't even know me in a year."

"She'll remember you. You're pretty hard to forget."

"How can someone just fuck up the next eighteen years of my life with no evidence?"

I could tell Levi's positive attitude was wearing thin when he put on his self-righteous face. "Lots of mothers are in dangerous situations," he said, like I needed a lecture.

"Being a mom doesn't make Eva a good person. She shouldn't be exempt from telling the truth."

Levi squinted at me. "Can you prove she was lying?"

"Obviously I can't, and no one would listen to me if I could, because I have a dick, so fuck me very much!"

That comment got the attention of some of the surrounding tables. Levi assured them that he was "handling me."

When did it become a problem to be pissed off at a bar, anyway?

"Did you present the parenting schedule like a human being?" Levi asked me.

"She wouldn't open the fucking door," I said, holding up the order. "Since the minute Sadie was born, Eva's been pushing me out of her life. So no, I didn't go groveling at her feet."

"Did you talk to the lawyer?"

"Didn't talk to him beforehand. Didn't talk to him after."

My brother leaned in, waiting for an explanation.

"Eva and Ryder were there," I told him. "It's two against one. There's no point in getting a lawyer 'cause I didn't file a police report when it happened, and I don't have any evidence."

Levi stood, pushing his iron chair back with a loud scrape. "Everything's ruined forever then, I guess."

I knew that tone. It meant he was done trying to reach me. And I don't know why, but it still made me feel guilty.

"Look, I know you're just trying to help. But this is my life now. Ryder is going to be the person Sadie looks up to, and next year I'll be the scary guy that picks her up on the weekends who she hates."

"I think you're making this worse than it needs to be," Levi said. "Don't drink too much tonight and don't skip work tomorrow. And for God's sake, talk to the lawyer and don't do anything stupid. I'll help you figure out the money stuff. We'll set up for a garage sale after work tomorrow."

# Monday Morning

The Dethbox shuddered as I swung into the parking lot, barely missing a Smart car. I checked the clock—7:57. In the mirror, the straw wrapper on my cheek reminded me of last night's blackout. No time to dwell. I wiped my face, ran my hands through my hair, and hurried into work.

The security guard lowered his glasses and glared at me. "Late again."

"Buzz me in," I said.

The guard, with all the grace of a dying turtle, pulled his logbook out and slid it across the counter. "Everybody needs to sign in."

"Seriously."

"Every morning," he said flatly.

The clock on the wall read 7:59. "Come on, I've got less than a minute."

His forehead crinkled. "Better sign quick."

I snatched the tethered pen from his desk, signed and dated the logbook, and added my manager's name:

**Davie Dickhead**

"That's not his name," the guard said.

I shot him a look. "You got a problem with me?"

"I've got a problem with people racing through my parking lot." He sniffed the air. "You come in here smelling like a damn bar with your shirt half-buttoned. My job is to make sure this place stays safe from people like you."

"People like me, huh?"

I grabbed the door handle and yanked on it until the old man buzzed me through. The wall of beige cubicles became a blur as I ran down the hall.

Without missing a beat, my boss, Davie, rounded the corner in his signature flannel shirt, tucked neatly into his dull khaki trousers, which accentuated his midsection bulge. He was wearing a punchable face that morning, clean-shaven, round like a child's, but lined with smug self-importance.

Davie fingered his sports watch. "You're part of the Valley of the Sun family, Zeke. We cover the phones from morning until night, and that means being logged into your computer on time, ready to go."

"I always work late," I said, taking a seat.

"Call centers rely on continuous phone coverage." Davie knelt. The sausage he must have pounded for breakfast overpowered the stale office air. "You need to respect your team members' time."

"I apologize, Davie," I said through gritted teeth.

He used my chair to push himself up. "Don't let it happen again."

As soon as Davie disappeared into his office, I escaped to the smoking patio to ask for a handout—my cigarettes had gone missing. It felt like a vise was tightening around my head. The tension was building up inside, making my temples throb.

Luckily, Damien was out on the patio, joking and laughing with people the way he did, making nice with everyone around him. I had to admire the charisma, and hope his goodwill extended to me.

"Can I bum a smoke?"

Damien grinned at me. "Rough night?"

"You have no idea."

"Tell you what, brother," he said as he pulled out an unopened pack of cigarettes. "If I can pack these suckers five millimeters deep, you're gonna let me help you."

"As long as I can bum one."

Damien beat the pack against his palm. Sharp knocks echoed through the smoking patio, each hitting louder than the last. Then he tore the plastic cover off and pulled one out.

"Oh, hell yeah," he said with a grin.

I snatched the cigarette and traced the pinstripes on the paper with my thumbnail. They were packed about seven deep.

"I'm throwing a party tonight," Damien continued. "Just for you."

"Tonight? ...it's Monday."

"So, call out Tuesday if you need to. It's not gonna be anything crazy though, just some friends hanging out."

# Hanging Out

Damien's offer wormed its way into my head. I drove to his address, but when I made it to the front door, I had to second-guess my decision. The thump of dubstep shook the walls. It was more than a couple of friends.

A voice inside my head told me to walk away, but a second, louder voice told me to stop being a little bitch and have some fun.

I opened the door. The house was like a scene out of an MTV Spring Break party. The girls outnumbered the guys three to one, and everyone was dancing. No lights, just blue and green glow sticks waving through the air.

"Monday night," I reminded myself as I stepped inside.

I needed to thank Damien for throwing a party together, but he had to know this wasn't my scene. I squeezed through the crowded living room until I reached the back wall, where he was posted up.

"How you gonna come to my place lookin' like that?" he asked.

I glanced at my ripped jeans and "So Far, So Good... So What!" t-shirt. Vic Rattlehead was covered in bullet belts and clutching an assault rifle. "Guess I'm the only thrasher here."

"Ain't nobody give a fuck about that," Damien said, shaking his head. "It's your face. That's the problem."

"What's wrong with my face?"

"You got that dumbass look on it, like you sad 'n shit."

I faked a smile, and Damien shook his head even more. "Nah, nuh-uh. Not here. Imma need you to take one of these." He reached in his pocket and pulled out a dime bag filled with red pills. A grin stretched across his face as he shook one into my hand. "Red Transformers."

"Ecstasy?"

Damien nodded. "On the house, brother."

"Thanks," I said. "But I've never done ecstasy."

A girl overheard us. She stopped dancing and approached me with wide, curious eyes.

"You've never rolled before?"

My gaze traced her stomach line down to a short, neon green skirt that barely covered her underwear. I stared for a minute, unable to look away as she moved her hips to the beat.

"Should I have?" I asked.

She nodded, still grooving to the music. "Get on my level."

I examined the pill more carefully, turning it over in my fingers. It was made to look like an Autobot from the old Transformers cartoon.

"These are safe?" I asked, looking around. "Everyone took one?"

"You'll be fine," she said as she grabbed my arm and dragged me to the kitchen. "Take it with orange juice. The vitamin C will make you roll harder."

The pill leached a bitter taste when I put it in my mouth. I pressed my eyes shut. Was I really about to take ecstasy?

"Relax," she said, handing me a glass.

Parents aren't supposed to drop ecstasy. I knew that. Hell, I've judged people for less, but what did it matter? I wasn't allowed to be a parent anymore. Those norms no longer applied to me. Everyone at the party was laughing, and dancing, and their faces were lit up with that stupid happy glow Damien always had.

So I said, "fuck it," and I knocked the pill back.

The girl grabbed my face and, with a loud "mwah," kissed me on the cheek. She had soft, inviting lips that left behind a layer of sticky gloss. I wanted to kiss her for real, but she pulled back.

"Name's Lez," she said as she walked away. "Give it thirty minutes to kick in, then come dance with me."

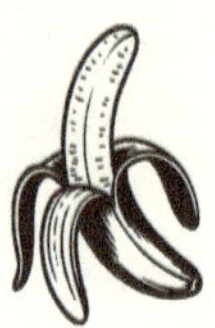

Thirty minutes later, I was still waiting for the drug to kick in. The EDM was jarring, my claustrophobia had gotten worse, and I wasn't any happier than I'd been before I took the pill.

All I'd done was watch Lez dance. We locked eyes a few times, but I didn't have the balls to talk to her until I could conjure a smile.

Meanwhile, Damien was slipping plastic rings on his fingers like a child as he bounced to the beat. Then he shooed some people off the couch and told me to sit down for a light show.

"You get Lez's number?" he asked.

"Nah," I said. "I don't think that's gonna work out."

"Thank God," Damien chuckled. "Leave that one alone if you know what's good."

"Why is that?"

Damien's plastic rings, it turned out, were light-ups. He switched them on one by one in preparation for his show, ignoring my question. I didn't push because the rings caught my attention. Each finger glowed with a different color: red thumbs, orange index fingers, yellow middles, green ring fingers, and blue pinkies.

He put his hands in the prayer position and waited for the next song.

As soon as the beat dropped, Damien's hands twisted. The colors blurred into vibrant halos that weaved hand over hand in a hypnotic display.

Like comets blazing across the night sky, the colors flowed around me, holding me in a trance. It wasn't just movement; it was art. The figure eights swirled into indistinguishable patterns, orbiting Damien's body.

In that moment, I didn't miss Sadie. Eva's bullshit didn't bother me, and Ryder didn't cross my mind. I wasn't even thinking about Damien, who was standing right in front of me, or Lez, the girl I'd been eye-banging for the past thirty minutes.

All I could think about were the colors, the beat, and the incredible feeling that was spreading through my nerve endings. It started at the base of my head, enveloped my skull, then shot through every fiber of my being. It was a feeling I had almost forgotten—happiness.

Sunlight filtered through the blinds. I blinked, then peeled myself off Damien's couch. That morning felt different. There was a sense of lightness to my body. Whiskey always left me feeling like I'd been beaten to the brink of death, but the morning after ecstasy was a calm, gentle awakening.

There was no anger, remorse, or depression. I felt a weird sense of peace, like things would be alright. The only mistake I made was not getting Lez's number. It'd be nice to have a friend like her.

A few guests were passed out on the floor. The girls all looked pretty similar—heavy eyeliner, scene haircuts, and short skirts—but I found Lez near the window. I flipped her over, and her tits fell out of her top.

"Yo!" Damien walked in. "Whatcha doin'?"

I jumped back and threw my hands up. "Just trying to get Lez's number."

"You think Lez got tits like dat?" Damien asked.

I glanced back at the girl, realizing she wasn't Lez. At least she didn't wake up. I tucked her cleavage away as tastefully as I could while Damien shook his head.

"You have Lez's number though, right?" I asked.

"I already told you," he said, taking on a serious tone. "You don't want that."

It was clear that he wasn't going to give me her number, and I let it go. Figured she was probably his ex or something. But there was another thing that I wanted from him, more than Lez's number.

"Can I buy some Transformers?"

"Fresh out," he said with a shrug. "And don't forget to call out of work."

A knot formed in my stomach, eating away at the delicate glow I'd woken up with. The ecstasy was incredible, but the thought that I might never experience joy again was terrifying.

"You can get more, right?"

"You can't roll every day," he said. "Gotta let that serotonin replenish."

I nodded, tensing my hand into a fist.

"Aight, fine," Damien said with a sigh of resignation. "You clearly need it. Just don't let it get the best of you. We'll head out once my dealer's up."

That's all I needed to hear. I dialed the office and waited. The security guard answered after a minute, and I gave him my best sick voice.

"I need to call out today."

"Sure, I can help you," he said. "Who's this?"

"Zeke Graves."

There was a sudden shift in his tone when he replied, "I should've known it was you."

Damien chuckled, mouthing the words, "Dude hates you."

"Okay, well this is like the first time I've ever called out of work." Frustration leaked into my voice. "Tell Davie the company will have to figure out a way to harass people without me for a day."

"I'll relay the message."

"Man, those assholes have it out for me," I said as I hung up.

"It's fifteen bucks a pill," Damien said. "Backslash don't do handouts."

I hadn't considered the cost of ecstasy. Fifteen bucks was more than I made an hour, which made happiness pretty damn expensive. I still had to pay rent, and Eva... But then it hit me. I wasn't allowed to contact Eva, and no one was garnishing my wages, so technically, I wasn't allowed to pay her.

"I've got the cash."

"Spoken like a mutha-fuckin' baller," he said with a grin.

Next thing I knew, we were on our way to meet some sketchy-ass drug dealer named Backslash. In hindsight, that should've been a red flag. Most people don't name themselves after diagonal lines. But I wasn't looking for normal people, chock-full of mundane routines and predictable results. I needed something more.

# Backslash

The Dethbox bottomed out on a speed bump. My mind wasn't on the road. It was on ecstasy, and the happiness I needed to buy. I made a mental budget. Since Damien said every three days is the max anyone should roll, I'd need ten pills a month.

"Call box," Damien shouted. "Stop."

I slammed on the brakes and rolled down the window. "What's the code?"

"6-8-3-2," he said.

The buttons were searing hot in the sunlight, and the green display was sun-bleached and cracked to the point where the numbers weren't visible. Nothing happened at first. No dial tones, or beeps, or sounds. Then a woman's voice crackled over the speaker.

"Watch your mouth, man," she said.

Damien leaned over me. "Say any damn thing I want, girl!"

I'd never heard of using movie quotes to screen people, but that wasn't the weirdest part. I had assumed Backslash was a dude. The type of sketchy-ass dude you could never be friends with but who could always get you what you needed.

"Backslash is a chick?"

Damien sat back in his seat. "Ya damn right."

"Okay, Shaft." I revved the engine and powered through the gate. "I can dig it."

We drove down the winding road, past a series of apartment buildings and tiny one-car garages, until we reached a big parking lot in the back. I pulled into an open spot, shifted into park, and jumped out.

Damien took the lead, guiding me to Backslash's building. Dry grass crunched under our feet. The place felt honest, raw, nothing like the fake, manicured park where Sadie and I used to play together. Here, the grass was dull and yellow. Patches of dirt dotted the field, and a lone circle of green sat beside a broken sprinkler where a scalding jet of water sprayed.

When we reached the unit, Damien knocked on the back door. Backslash answered quickly. Her sparkling eyeshadow and black dress were intense, and the tattoos reaching up her shoulders led the eyes down.

"Is he some kind of creep?" she asked.

"He's cool," Damien said. "He just thinks you're hot."

Backslash squinted at me. "What's your name, cool guy?"

"Ze—"

Damien shushed me. "How you gonna give some random dealer your name? The less we all know about each other, the better."

"I'm Graves," I said.

Telling her my last name wasn't better, but it's the first thing I blurted out, and it kind of stuck. Backslash stepped aside and let us in. Her place looked like a Spencer's. The hall was lit with black lights and covered in psychedelic posters. She led us down the hall and past a couple of empty rooms until we got to hers.

"Your place is pretty legit."

Backslash took a lockbox from her closet. "Thanks," she said, jumping onto her bed, "As long as you like it, Graves." Then she took a silver key off the nightstand and opened the box. The left side was stuffed with pills, and the right side was filled with cash. "What'll it be?"

I fished my wallet out. "Two Transformers?"

"Sixty bucks."

I turned to Damien. "You said fifteen each."

"Is he the fucking dealer?" Backslash's gentle tone took a harsh turn.

"I—"

"I don't know you," she said. "Your price is thirty."

My heart sank. The entire budget I'd worked out in my head just got shot to shit. Ten pills at thirty bucks a pop came to three hundred a month. That was like buying a brand-new car.

"What can I do to get the friend discount?"

"Damien doesn't drive," Backslash said, eyeing me. "I assume you've got wheels."

"Yeah."

"Then be my friend, Graves."

"Like, help you sell drugs or something?"

Backslash nodded.

"I've got a kid," I told her. "I can't really get mixed up in that stuff."

"You can drop ecstasy though?" she asked, looking at me like I was crazy.

"A little."

Backslash slammed her lockbox shut. "Look guy, I've got a business to run here. If you don't want to pay full price, then be my friend. Otherwise, stop wasting my time and pay up."

She didn't see it this way, but there was a line in the sand between being a drug dealer and wanting to feel happy sometimes. But I wasn't about to walk away empty-handed, so I paid her sixty bucks.

Damien tapped my shoulder. "Give me your phone."

I didn't know why, but I handed it over.

"This is Backslash's number," he said, punching in the digits. "She likes you."

I glanced at Backslash. She returned an intense and fiery stare as she packaged the Transformers. Meanwhile, Damien slid the back off my phone, took out the battery pack, and tossed it to me. Then he took the pills from Backslash, hid them in the battery compartment, and secured the back in place.

"Right on, Slash," Damien said. "We out."

Having the pills gave me a sense of security, but I knew they wouldn't last long. I had to rework my budget. There were cutbacks that would be beneficial, anyway. Drinking was one of them. After all, I had an entire year to keep myself sane before I could see Sadie again.

"Graves is a pretty dope name," Damien said as he stepped into the Dethbox.

I shook my head to clear the mental fog around Sadie, then got into the driver's seat. "Well, he *is* a bad mother—"

"Shut yo' mouth."

I shifted into drive with a big smirk on my face. "But I'm talking about Shaft."

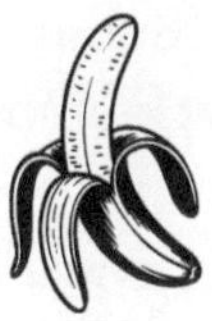

Returning home that night was a bummer. I liked being Graves, and I hesitated for a moment before unlocking the door. I knew Levi was going to pissed off and give me a hard time about not setting up that garage sale with him.

Levi was everything I wasn't, a constant reminder that I wasn't good enough. It wasn't just his do-gooder attitude that bothered me. It was the house too. The rent was out of control and the drive to work was agonizing.

I just didn't want to do it anymore.

"Where have you been?" Levi asked when I walked in.

"Out."

"And you don't answer your fucking phone!" He threw his hands up. "You never came home last night."

"Have you just been waiting for me like a jilted wife?"

"I called your work, and you weren't there. So, I've been waiting the required amount of time to file a missing person's report."

"Why are you like this? I asked.

"Because I'm the one who has to take care of you," he said. "Did you black out again?"

I blew in his self-righteous face. "I didn't drink."

It felt like he wanted me to have drank though. Like he was just sitting around, angry, waiting to lecture me.

"Call next time," Levi said.

I took my phone out, figuring I would show him that it was dead, but the battery pack fell out of my pocket.

"Why would you take the battery out?" he asked, tilting his head.

"I dropped it," I told him. "It won't stay on."

He held his hand out. "Bullshit, let me take a look."

I shoved the phone back in my pocket. "It's just busted. Why do you always assume I'm up to something?"

"Because I know you," Levi said, blocking my path. "When mom was sick, who raised you? I know when you're lying to me, and I know when you're hiding things. It's my job to keep you safe."

"Maybe you didn't get the memo, but I'm a big boy now."

Levi reached into my pocket and stole the phone. I grabbed his arm, and before I knew it, our little spat turned into a full-on brawl. We hit the ground. Both of us had our hands on the phone as we rolled across the floor, crashed into the ladder shelf, and watched it wobble.

Only one thing fell, a picture of our mom, and it shattered.

I let go of the phone and let Levi check the back.

"Drugs?" He looked at me, repulsed. "You're gonna get yourself arrested."

"Calm your tits, dude."

Levi jumped to his feet and started pacing, unsure what to do. His tits were decidedly not calm, and he had no intentions of subduing them.

"What are you thinking?" he asked.

"Just give me my pills back."

Instead of listening to reason, Levi took off down the hall.

I chased him into the bathroom, just to watch him throw my pills in the toilet and flush them. Without hesitation, I plunged my hands into the bowl, but the bag slipped through my fingers and disappeared down the pipes.

"Look at yourself," he said. "That's disgusting."

I punched him with a fistful of toilet water. "Do you know how much that shit cost?"

Levi shoved me back. "Not as much as the rent costs."

I gave him the finger, stormed into my room, and slammed the door. Happiness was a distant memory at that point. I was officially back to being Zeke—anxious, sad, and beat-down. Every night I passed out alone, and every morning I woke up to the same tired disaster.

# The Grind

Traffic was bumper to bumper that morning. By the time I found a parking spot, I was almost late. I switched off the radio. My attention shifted to the digital display—7:57.

How long could I keep doing this?

The guard at the front desk glared as I walked past, but I barely noticed.

"Buzz me in," I said, grabbing the door handle.

He shifted his glasses like he didn't recognize me. "But you don't work here anymore."

I glared back at him, feeling my patience shrink. "I'm not in the mood."

"Maybe you didn't understand me." The guard stood tall. "This is a right-to-work state. When you didn't call out of work yesterday, Davie found a way to harass people without you, permanently."

I stepped up to his desk. "That's bullshit, I called you."

"Really?" He scratched his head and looked around. "I don't remember that."

"I have the record in my phone."

The guard sat back down, grinning. "So maybe you did call." He clasped his hands and rested his chin on his knuckles. "Maybe you called and threatened me. You sounded drunk, or high. Let me tell you something, this is my building. I identify threats and I get rid of them."

"More like you and Davie get rid of people you don't like."

I was beginning to understand how the world worked, and how people viewed me. As if I, a "drunken, abusive father," could win this battle. I wasn't getting my job back, and I didn't want it back, either. It was a sign to move on. I dialed Backslash from the lobby. Being Zeke was no longer a sustainable option. It was time to be someone else, someone more exciting.

"Hey, it's Graves," I said into the receiver. "If you need a friend, then let's get started."

# Getting Started

The sun beat down as I knocked on Backslash's door. Ten minutes passed with no answer, but I'd spoken with her on the phone just thirty minutes ago.

I pressed my face against the windowpane. The lights were off inside, except the black light in the hall. Its ultraviolet glow tinted the glass purple.

My future and happiness were inside, just waiting for me. I turned the doorknob and found the door was unlocked. "Hey," I called out as the door creaked open. "It's me, Graves."

Brisk air wafted out, inviting me in. A reasonable person would have walked away, but I wasn't feeling reasonable. I checked behind me, saw there was no one around, and snuck inside to investigate.

"The door was open," I said as I walked down the hall.

When I reached Backslash's bedroom, she was lying face down on the bed, wrapped in a plush blanket. I crept up next to her and shook her shoulder.

"Hey, Backslash. You okay?"

I put my ear to her mouth, but she wasn't breathing.

"Wake up," I said, clapping my hands.

She choked and stirred but didn't get up. At least she was alive.

"I have money," I told her, even though she was out cold.

It didn't look like we were going to be getting started any time soon, but I needed some of those pills. I knew where she kept the lock box so I grabbed it from the closet and took the silver key from her nightstand.

"I'm gonna take two Transformers and leave the cash, I'll hit you up later."

Backslash's eyes shot open. She grabbed my wrist.

"Jesus!" my heart pounded. "What the actual fuck Slash?"

She took my cash and counted it. "Sixty, good."

"Were you awake the whole time?" I asked, catching my breath. "Not cool."

Backslash sat up, clear-eyed and cognizant. The black dress she wore the other day still clung to her curves. Her fingers dug into my wrist as she pulled me to the bed next to her.

"You learn more about druggies when they think you're asleep."

"Then you know I'm legit," I said.

Backslash let go of my wrist. "You're honest for having the cash, but you're a fiend for letting yourself in." Her gaze shifted to my necklace, and the crucifix pendant that hung from it. "Some kinda weird, metalhead, Jesus freak hippie, who likes to trespass in my apartment."

"The door was open..."

With a slow, deliberate look, Backslash sighed, "You'd turn on me in a second."

"I wouldn't."

"It's not a matter of if, just when."

"The door was open, you obviously expected me to walk in. And I brought cash, what's not to trust?"

"What if you were broke, and you knew where my stash was?"

She was talking to me the way I talked to the debtors at Valley of the Sun, there was no faith behind her words, only a disbelief in decency.

"You can trust me."

"Talk is cheap." she said, opening the lockbox. "Notice anything missing?"

The box, which had been stuffed to the brim with drugs and cash the other day, was almost empty.

"Most of the pills," I said. "And the money."

Her gaze dropped before snapping back at me. "You can't trust people, Graves. You think you can, but you can't." She opened the remaining drug bags one by one, gathering the leftover pills and collecting them in one larger bag. "I got jacked. I gotta make some money."

"That's why I'm here."

"You're here to get high, but you'll need to help me too."

Backslash took a mirror from her nightstand. Then she took a handful of empty bags and shook the colorful residue from each of them onto the mirror's surface. "There's a rave tonight," she said, pulling a card from her pocket. "Boo's Warehouse on Jackson and Fourth."

"Are you going?"

Backslash used her license to divide the powder into fine lines. "Fuck no."

My neck twitched as I eyed the colorful lines. Chemical reactions started firing in my brain, priming me for the rush of ecstasy.

"You're going," she said, handing me a rolled-up bill. "You're gonna sell my pills."

"Let's start slow. I've never been to a rave."

"There's no such thing as slow, Graves. Move the rest of my pills tonight at forty bucks a pop, then you can be my dealer."

It was pretty obvious that I was only going to get the freebie line if I said yes to her. That was a turning point, my chance to make money, buy unlimited happiness, and get out of this mental funk.

The old Zeke would've bitched out, but he was a pussy. I took the dirty bill, shoved it up my nose, and snorted a line of rainbow drug dust. The burn shot up my nostril, searing my brain with a sudden, violent pain that only intensified, peaking in a white-hot blaze, before a tidal wave of euphoria crashed down.

When my breathing leveled out, my doubts had subsided. I was ready for a warehouse rave in downtown Phoenix.

# Rave Girl

Smoke poured from the DJ booth, distorting the lights and swirling around the ravers' heads. The warehouse pulsed with pink neon beams. Beneath the flashing colors, a sea of bodies moved to the electronic beat. Everywhere I looked, there were glow sticks, homemade kandi bracelets, and flashing binkies.

It was objectively awesome, but smuggling pills in put a damper on my high. There were bags everywhere, including in my underwear. I had to pop a Transformer to keep the tension at bay. And I needed it to hit me hard, so I chewed it instead of swallowing, enduring the bitter chemical taste.

I took Damien with me too. He was holding half of the pills and agreed to coach me in return for a Transformer. He hadn't done anything but get distracted though, and he didn't bother to intervene when a raver skipped up to me holding a Vicks inhaler.

"Seabreeze?" she asked, like I knew what that was.

She wore white fur boots, pink stockings, and a rainbow skirt that didn't come close to covering her underwear. I couldn't choke out a response, and before I could react, she put the inhaler in her mouth and blew into it—a blast of icy menthol burned my corneas like acid.

"You're rolling, right?" she asked, confused by my horrified reaction.

I wiped the burning tears from my face. "Yeah, so?"

She pulled a Canon camera out of her bra and took a picture of me. "Oh my God, your face right now. I'm so posting this on DontStayIn."

With that, she skipped away.

Damien was laughing hysterically. “You good, brother?”

Surprisingly, I was good. As the vaporized droplets lost their sting, I felt fresh and invigorated. My roll was stronger and more pleasant than before.

“I guess so, but you’re supposed to be teaching me about this shit.”

“Move two pills to your front pocket,” he said. “Raves ain’t what they used to be. We’re not gonna get raided ’cause the cops are already here, undercover. If you get caught, apologize, and give up the decoy pills in your front pocket.”

“These aren’t decoys, Damien. They’re real.”

“Two pills is personal use. The cops don’t care. Shit, half these kids are underage. The cops are here to take down drug dealers, so don’t let them find out that you’re selling. If they think you just here to roll, they’ll let you go.”

Tension was sneaking through my high. “What if I sell to an undercover?”

Damien laughed. “Don’t sell to old-ass motherfuckers. Sell to the rolly kids in cuddle puddles rubbin’ each other.”

“Show me how.”

“For a cut,” Damien said, upping his initial one pill fee. “Ten bucks per sale.”

I had to take that into consideration. Backslash trusted me to sell her pills, but she never counted them, she’d combined the bags while she was talking to me. So, I agreed to Damien’s terms with the assumption that, as long as I went back with a stack of cash, she’d never know he got a cut.

Just as soon as I agreed, the DJ dropped a new track, and the crowd surged. Everyone knew the words, “I know this pretty rave girl, always think about her.” After that, the beat took hold, and the crowd surrounded us. I lost Damien in the shuffle, but I spotted Lez dancing to the song.

"Hey!" she broke out of the crowd and rushed over. "You're the guy from the party."

It felt like fate. "Name's Graves," I said. "I never got your number."

"Well, that was pretty stupid, wasn't it?" She held her hand out. "Give me your phone."

"Come back," her friends yelled.

Lez stared at her waiting hand. "What are you waiting for? Give me your phone. I'm putting my number in it."

She punched in her number and then ran off, leaving me alone to search for Damien. I found him behind the warehouse approaching two younger-looking guys. A whispered word and a nod were all it took for him to make the sale. I watched to see how the handoff worked.

Instead, the three of them all walked to the porta-john together and took turns inside. After the last guy finished up, they all chatted for a bit, and then Damien came and found me.

"See that shit?" he asked.

"No."

Damien brushed the imaginary dirt off his shoulder. "First dude left the cash in the john. Then I took the cash and left the pills. Then the last dude went in and got the pills. That's all there is to it, brother. Keep it loose."

That was the first of many techniques Damien shared with me. We spent the rest of the rave practicing how to stay loose. Damien picked the buyers and devised schemes, and I carried them out. At first, I was stiff. People didn't trust me. But once I loosened up, I made sales. Because the key to selling isn't being good at it, it's belonging. And I fucking belonged.

# Tricky Bitch

Backslash's stare cut through me. "Where are the rest of my pills?"

She was still wearing that slutty black dress, and I was sure she hadn't washed it. Did her room always smell this funky?

"Well?" she asked.

Okay, I needed to stop judging Backslash and focus on the problem at hand—I bought Damien's help last night using her cash, and somehow, she knew about it. She didn't know exactly what had happened, but she knew I was lying to her.

"Like I said, I sold the pills at price."

Backslash's pointer finger carried invisible numbers through the air. "You brought me eight hundred and ten," she said. "Twenty-seven pills at forty a pop is a thousand and eighty." She set the cash down on her bed and locked eyes with me. "And you said I could trust you."

There was no going back, so I doubled down. "There weren't that many pills."

"Do you think I'm some dumb bitch?"

I know a trap when I see one. I kept my mouth shut, but Backslash didn't let up.

"Do. You. Think. That I... am a dumb bitch?"

"No."

"Then why would I give a complete stranger all of my drugs without counting them?"

She wasn't a dumb bitch. She was a tricky bitch. From the moment I called her, she'd been conducting tests. She wanted reassurance, not just about my ability to handle drug dealing, but about my integrity. Her actions were deliberate. She had counted the pills before I arrived yesterday, and she sent me to the rave to see if I would return with the right amount.

"Were you even robbed?" I asked.

"Please." Backslash rolled her eyes. "People know better."

Backslash was a pro, and if I wanted this job, she needed to believe I could sell drugs on my own, that I didn't waste her time.

"The price was way too high. No one was paying forty."

"You discounted my pills?"

I nodded.

In truth, I sold them at forty, minus Damien's cut. I hated lying to Backslash. It went against everything I stood for, but I needed her to believe that I could handle this job.

"Thirty isn't a discount," I said. "People were selling for twenty."

"You get what you pay for," Backslash muttered. "Sorry, Graves, this isn't gonna work."

"I was under the impression you got robbed," I said, digging in deeper. "You've lied to me twice, and I thought it would be better to come back with something instead of nothing."

Backslash's posture softened. "Don't do it again."

The tension in the room thinned, but the unease in my gut intensified. My mom taught me not to lie, so why did it come out so easily? I lied to protect myself, to trick her into thinking I was someone I wasn't. How was I still looking at her? Why was she still staring through me?

"Are we good?" I asked.

Backslash got out of bed and threw a denim jacket over her shoulder. "As soon as you pay back the two seventy you owe me." Then she grabbed lip gloss, a makeup palette, and a wad of cash and tossed them into her studded pink purse. "Lucky for you, it's time to re-up."

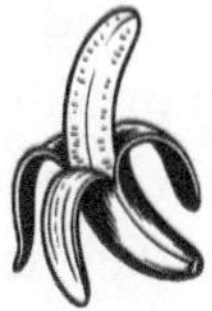

The Dethbox's headlights cast a weak, yellow glow on the asphalt. My attention was divided between the hookers loitering on the corner and Backslash. She had one foot up on the dash, her slutty black dress was hiked up, and she was counting her cash.

The light flipped from red to green, and I took off. We were picking up a "boat," which I learned that night was a thousand pills, and that felt real. More real than stuffing pills in my underwear.

"What if we get pulled over?" I asked.

"Don't," Backslash said, pausing her count. "Unless you wanna die in prison."

"And you only pay a thousand bucks for a boat?"

Backslash pocketed the cash and stared at me. "You ask a lot of questions, Graves."

"I'm freakin' out a little."

"Turn here," she said; it was all old news to her.

I made a hard right into the neighborhood, then checked the rearview mirror for cops. She could've at least directed me sooner. The last thing we needed was to get pulled over in this part of town.

"If you pay one dollar a pill," I said. "Why do I pay thirty?"

"Because drugs are how I make money," she said, directing me to pull through a tight alleyway. "You're earning your friend discount tonight, and I'll toss you some freebies to get started."

The Dethbox forced its way through a mess of tangled weeds, which sprouted through the chain-link backyard fences surrounding us. Pavement gave way to gravel. Broken glass crunched under our tires. In the glow of the headlights, a pile of damaged appliances, toys, and pallets revealed itself.

"Park here," Backslash ordered.

The brakes whined as we rolled to a stop. I cut the engine, then the lights. Wind blew dead weeds against the hood while I kept an eye out in every direction.

"What now?"

Backslash hiked her dress up further. "We wait."

Her pussy was basically staring me in the face. I didn't know if that was an invitation or not, but I didn't take it if it was. Rustling leaves caught my attention just before a cat with glowing eyes jumped onto the Dethbox's hood. My nerves were shot by the time Backslash cracked her window and whistled into the darkness.

A man approached, his hands shoved deep in his hoodie pocket. Backslash stuck her money out the window. The man snatched it, then he peered past Backslash to get a better look at me and grunted. He was a gruff, older Hispanic man. His weathered and expressionless eyes stared into mine.

"Two grand," he said.

"What the fuck, Miguel?" Backslash showed no fear.

"You bring him to make me jealous?" Miguel asked, and that's when I realized she was hiking her dress up for him. "You're lucky I don't skin your bitch ass," he said. "Fucking ho."

Backslash batted her eyes at me. "Guess he's threatened by you, Graves."

My knuckles went white clutching the wheel. What the fuck was she thinking? Miguel had the first thousand in his pocket, and he was dangling the heavy-duty Ziplock bag of pills in front of the window.

"Maybe I make it three grand," he said.

Backslash pulled another thousand from her wallet. "Two or he'll run your ass down."

Miguel took her cash and tossed the pills in the car, gave her both middle fingers, then vanished just as quickly as he had appeared, and all I could hear after that was my heartbeat.

"What the hell was that?" I asked Backslash.

"We used to hook up," she said, pulling her dress down. "He thinks he's hard cause he works with the cartel, but he's a little bitch. He hates it when I'm with anyone, and I like fucking with him."

"He works for a drug cartel?"

She tilted her head. "You know drugs come from criminals, right?"

"Maybe don't tell those criminals that I'm gonna run them down or make them think I'm sleeping with you."

"Oh my God, don't be such a little bitch."

"I think I'm in over my head," I said as I turned the engine over and pushed through the alleyway. "I'll pay you back the two seventy, then I'm out."

"Bringing you in just cost me an extra grand." She pushed the pills under her seat while keeping her eyes on me. "You're just stressed. Take a day, call a bitch you like, fuck it out."

# A Bitch I Liked

Lez knocked on my door. I ran my hands through my hair, took a breath, and then answered. Backslash was right. I needed to have some fun and Lez was the person to call. Of course, Levi wouldn't approve, so I made sure to plan around his work schedule.

"Are you gonna let me in?" Lez asked.

I peered past her at the car driving away. "Who was that?"

"My ride."

The driver looked like a girl from what I could see, which was ideal. I was hoping Lez wouldn't get dropped off by some dude, especially not in that outfit. She strutted through the door in the shortest denim shorts I'd ever seen and had a top on that looked more like a belt.

"I'm glad you could come," I said, steering her to the kitchen.

She admired the bag of pills I'd left out on the table. "Green guns," she said instantly identifying them.

"Yeah, no big deal."

If we're being honest, I left that shit out to impress her. To let her know that I could get her what she wanted. At least there were a few freebies I could share.

I was a little bummed that they weren't Transformers. These pills were basic, a standard circular shape, with a gun imprint on both sides. Either way, they were going to get pulverized. Snorting hit so much harder.

I sat down at the table, opened the bag, and pulled out a couple of pills, but I couldn't continue—not on the kitchen table. There was this weird knot in my stomach, kind of like the one I got when I lied to Backslash. For some reason, using the kitchen table felt criminal, and even talking about dealing in the house was weird.

"On second thought," I said, grabbing the bag. "My room."

My heart was racing as we walked down the hall. Lez's ass jiggled beneath the frayed denim threads as she strutted past me into the room. I threw the bag in the nightstand drawer and got to crushing the freebies with my license. Then I divvied out two lines and rolled up a twenty for her to use.

"Ladies first."

Her voice was low and seductive as she slid the twenty from my hand. "Is it just the two of us tonight?"

I nodded.

She bent over the nightstand with her back arched and snorted a line. She choked, and I couldn't look away from that heart-shaped ass as it shook.

"I can usually take the whole thing," she pouted. Then her lips curled into a smile, her teeth just grazing the edge of the words she whispered to me. "Unless you like it when I gag."

I ran my hand over her hip, feeling the curve of her body beneath my fingertips. Then I leaned over the nightstand and snorted my line. Lez had her top off when I turned around. Her pierced nipples were erect, her gaze locked on mine, her breath warm on my face as our lips hovered inches apart.

She reached her hands under my shirt.

Ecstasy heightened every sensation, and the mere touch of her fingers sent shivers down my spine. A pleasant warmth bloomed on my skin and followed the trail of her fingers.

"I wanna make my ex jealous," Lez said, getting her phone.

While I tore my pants off, she got comfortable on her knees. Blood rushed through my veins as her fingers tightened around my dick. The pressure built as her tongue teased me. I couldn't wait for her to get her camera ready. I pushed her head down until she choked on it.

"Wait," she gasped.

She pursed her lips, held her phone out, and gave my dick a kiss.

Then she went down again. I pulled her head back, leaving a glistening strand of saliva stretching from her lips to the tip of my dick.

"I guess you do like it when I gag," she said. "So did he." She picked her phone off the ground and texted the picture to her ex. "If you met Ryder, you'd get why I hate him so much."

My blood ran cold. "Ryder?"

She started bobbing on my dick again, but I pushed her off.

"What does Ryder look like?"

"Are you into dudes or something?" she asked. "I mean... could be fun."

"No, it's probably a coincidence," I said as my dick started going soft. "My bitch of an ex is dating a Ryder."

"Well, he's ginger." She stroked my dick, trying to keep it hard while she went on. "Pale, freckled, his hair is kinda light." Then she shook her head. "He knocked up some bitch while we were dating and wanted to keep hooking up with me. I mean, we did. But that's not the point."

Lez went down on me again, but I was losing juice. It's almost impossible to be upset on ecstasy, and somehow the mood started to sour. Anger crept in, the memories of betrayal lingered, but the rage was being overwritten in real time. I was infuriated, but unable to react right, and then it hit me.

I hadn't thought about Sadie at all.

Did I even have a daughter, or had I been raising Ryder's kid? Is that why I didn't matter to Eva, and why Ryder was able to steal my life from under me? I needed it to make sense.

"Are you like, okay?" Lez was still on her knees, holding my limp dick.

She sucked on the tip until I was hard again. The serotonin and dopamine cleansed my mind of negativity and kept my stress under control. Kind of. I grabbed the back of Lez's head and fucked her throat so hard her makeup smeared down her slutty, tear-streaked face.

"What the fuck, bro?" Levi burst into the bedroom.

I threw Lez to the floor and covered my dick with a pillow. "Why are you home?"

Lez was on her back with saliva running from her mouth down to her tits. "You're next," she said, eyeing Levi.

Levi had one of my pills pinched between his fingers. It must've fallen out.

"It's a good thing I got off early," he said. "I should've known this shit wasn't just gonna blow over. This whole year I let you fuck around, but I told you no drugs in the fucking house."

I pulled my pants up and confronted Levi. "Get out of my room."

"Get out of my house." He shoved me back. "And take the slut with you."

At least he didn't know about the massive bag of pills, or he might've shit himself. That fight had been a long time coming, anyway. I pulled Lez to her feet and threw my clothes on. We needed to find a place to finish what we started, and then I had to find a new roommate.

# GOOD GIRL

## ERINN

Erinn applied a thick stroke of kohl liner to the underside of her eye. She slipped, smearing the liner, wiped it off, and reapplied. Then she leaned into the vanity mirror, teased her bangs, and sprayed a bright yellow bottle of göt2b glued until the room was a synthetic, fruity haze.

"Ready yet?" her roommate Chels asked.

"Almost."

She could never get her hair to hold before leaving. It always looked perfect when she had nowhere to go. But no matter how long she straightened it, if she had to be somewhere, a stray curl would always pop up.

The way Chels asked if she was 'ready yet' felt like a pointed accusation disguised as a question. What she was really asking was, "Are you going to the party or are you going to break down and bail on me?"

Erinn met Chels' eyes in the mirror. "I said I'm going."

"The guys from IWatchedHerDie are gonna be there," Chels said. "We can't be late, or some other chick is gonna be all up in their business."

Erinn dropped her hairspray and spun around. "Do I look okay?"

Chels nodded. "Totally scene."

Erinn ran to her closet and pulled out two shirts. One was The Used, with the iconic heart noose logo from In Love and Death. And the other, My Chemical Romance, The Black Parade with the marching skeleton.

"Or do I go retro?" she asked, adding her Kurt Cobain suicide note shirt to the mix.

Chels eyed Erinn, noting her skinny jeans and spiked belt. "The Used, for sure."

"Do lots of people in their twenties go to house parties?" Erinn asked as she removed her current top and replaced it with her Used shirt. "Oh, dear god my hair! I'm gonna scream."

"What part of IWatchedHerDie didn't you hear?"

"I'm not going there to hook up," Erinn said through another cloud of göt2b glued.

"Which is why you don't need to be this stressed out about your hair. It looks hot. You look hot. I'd fuck you. But I'm going to be busy." Chels walked up to Erinn and squeezed her shoulder. "Maybe take off the Jesus necklace. It doesn't really fit with the vibe you're rockin."

"Are you ever gonna stop giving me crap?"

"Keep it tucked," Chels said. "You're never gonna meet guys like that."

"Again, not trying to."

Chels smiled. "I'm excited to party with you, though."

"Why'd you say it like that?" Erinn asked, tousling her hair in the mirror.

"Like what?

Erinn glared at Chels' reflection. "Really?"

Chels tilted her head to the side. "It's just, you know, you never really go out with me."

Erinn gave up on her hair and collapsed on her bed, strewn among a pile of rejected clothes. She wasn't a party girl, and she never had been. Loud music and crowded rooms made her anxious. Sure, she liked the music and the scene, but she was a good girl. The type of girl who stayed in on Friday nights, said a prayer before meals, and curled up with a book.

"I just wanna forget about my ex for a night," she said.

Chels sat down next to Erinn. "We're going to have fun. I'll look out for you. I promise."

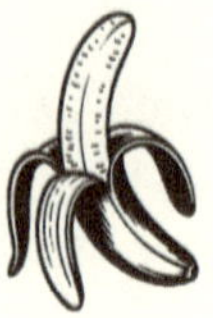

When they arrived, the house party had already spilled onto the front lawn. Cigarette smoke rose in clouds above the crowd. Choppy layers, side-swept bangs, and tight pants as far as the eye could see.

Erinn drove around the cul-de-sac. The street was lined with cars squeezed in bumper to bumper, forcing her to drive further down the block.

"Seriously," Chels smacked her forehead on the window as more guests hurried past them towards the party. "Look at all these people. No way I'm getting to hang with the band."

Erinn wrestled her Smart car into a tight space between a beat-up, rust-white Toyota Corolla and a dented, navy-blue Honda Accord.

She and Chels jumped out of the car and ran to the party. Erinn was overcome with the cigarette smoke. Tightness seized her lungs, making her cough. Chels let out a derisive snort, and Erinn knew she'd need to suck it up and deal with the smell. Nobody wanted to hang out with the girl who couldn't hack it. This was her night to prove she could survive at a real party.

She took the lead and opened the front door. The house was so full that they couldn't move, and the smoke inside, with nowhere to dissipate, was worse than outside. There were speakers in the corner blasting All That Remains so loud they couldn't hear themselves think.

"You must hate this," Chels yelled.

Erinn put her face up to Chels' ear. "Are you getting in there or what?"

"I'm sweating my ass off."

"Maybe we should go outside until things die down," Erinn suggested.

They hugged the wall, inching their way around the massive crowd until they were able to squeeze themselves out the back door. Erinn could tell Chels disliked the party as much as she did, even though she'd never admit it. The two ended up slumped against the outside wall, with the beat vibrating the stucco, watching people smoke and drink, while they talked.

# The Party

## Graves

Damien put his hand on a stranger's shoulder, and with a whisper in his ear, the guy stepped aside, letting us reach the keg. The crowd was a mix of metalheads, emos, screamos, and scene kids, and somehow a group of bros still dominated the keg.

Even though it wasn't Damien's scene, he fit in better than I did. The dude was a social chameleon, who could navigate any crowd. He grabbed two Solo cups and started pumping the keg until the handle was stiff.

"You sellin' tonight?" Damien asked.

I knew why he was asking. Sales had been slow since the rave, and I was going to need to cough up rent for crashing on his couch. Levi had called me a couple of weeks ago to make amends, but I ignored him.

"Backslash's prices are too high," I said. "Even her existing clients are leaving. They all get pills for fifteen to twenty."

Damien handed me a cup. "I could sell a thirty-dollar pill to anybody here."

"Oh yeah, who would you sell to?"

Damien looked around the yard for a suitable candidate. He zeroed in on two girls who were standing with their backs against the wall. "Those girls," he said. "No question about it."

One was a short, heavyset girl, wearing black stockings and a too-small skirt. A devil-horned headband pushed back her thick black hair, tugging at her penciled-on eyebrows. The other girl was tall and thin, with tight jeans, aggressive spiked hair, and an old Used shirt.

"Why them?" I asked, my gaze lingering on the girl in the Used shirt.

"They don't belong here," Damien said. "You can tell by how they standing. All stiff and uncomfortable. They don't know what to say, don't know what to do. They'd buy pills just to impress you."

"That feels wrong."

"Where do you draw the line, brother? There ain't no free rides here, you want to keep crashin' at my place, you gotta make money. You signed up to do all the stuff that dude on your necklace don't like."

Lines existed. They were just scattered. Certain places were okay, certain people were okay. Others weren't. Selling drugs to ravers at a warehouse was better than selling to two loners at a party. Just like doing drugs at Damien's place was better than doing them at Levi's.

In any case, I didn't have leeway to argue. I left Damien and approached the girls, who quickly spotted me coming towards them. The rest of the walk became an awkward game of look-away.

"The fuck do you want?" The heavy-set girl said, coming in hot.

I put my hands up. "Just sayin hi."

"Don't worry," her friend said. "She's harmless, just bummed the band is busy."

"I'm Graves," I said, extending my hand.

The girl in the Used shirt took my hand and shook it dramatically, like I was ridiculous for offering a handshake. "I'm Erinn," she said, then, looking at her friend with a smile, she added, "This is Chels."

"Nice to meet you."

Chels responded with an eye roll and shifted away from me.

I didn't feel like I belonged at that party, not the way I'd belonged at the rave, and the girls didn't seem like the 'sure thing' that Damien had pegged them as. There must've been a better way, but I went in direct and to the point.

"Do you girls like ecstasy?"

Chels grasped Erinn's arm and pulled her inside the house. Meanwhile, Damien gave a mocking slow clap as I headed back to the keg empty-handed.

"It's not my fault," I told him. "Not everyone wants to buy drugs."

With that, Damien shrugged and walked away, absorbing into a random clique. He did that from time to time, seamlessly melding with a party and enjoying himself. Meanwhile, I identified more with the two girls standing against the wall.

Then I got a reminder I wasn't looking for, a text from Eva.

> I hear you're hanging around Ryder's ex.
> Tell that ho to back off.

I almost responded, which would've been a big mistake considering the order and the communication restrictions, but Erinn, the girl in the Used shirt, saved me when she snuck up behind me and tapped me on the shoulder.

"Fill me up," she said, waving her red Solo cup in my face.

"Sorry about earlier," I said, pumping the keg.

"Chels is just protective," Erinn said. "But she's trying to hang with the band now."

Erinn pulled a necklace out from under her shirt. It was a crucifix just like mine. She smiled at me and asked if we could be buddies. She was a little weird, but I returned her cup and told her we already were.

"What does it feel like?" she asked, taking a sip of beer. "Ecstasy."

"What's the happiest you've ever felt?"

She closed her eyes and smiled wide. "When I got my first puppy, Chloe. She was so cute and little, and her nose hadn't come in yet."

"Multiply that feeling by a thousand."

"That sounds amazing," she said, downing her cup in a single gulp. "I haven't felt new-puppy happy for a long time. Everything is so heavy. Work and struggling to get by. Things with my ex. Life was more fun back before this whole real-life thing. I don't know what fun is now."

This girl would buy from me, I realized, but should she?

"Ecstasy isn't for everyone," I told her.

Erinn didn't know what she was asking for, but she asked anyway. "Is it for me?"

"No."

"Don't you want me to be happy, Graves?" she asked, shaking her cup for a refill.

I filled both of our cups, and we ended up talking for so long that we each had a couple more refills. When she asked me about the pills again, I was too far gone to consider the line, and whether I was crossing it. All I knew was this girl wanted to roll with me, and that sounded amazing.

"First one's on me," I said, taking her hand.

We forced our way through the crowd until we reached a tiny bathroom nestled under the stairs. It was tight inside, face to face. We were so close I couldn't smell anything but the product in her hair. Her eyes popped through a layer of thick black liner, looking sweet and innocent. I reached in my pocket and pulled out the ecstasy.

"Just half for me," she said.

I split a pill in half, gave part to her, then swallowed mine with a sip of beer. It wasn't going to be a profitable night, but it would be fun. Within half an hour, we transitioned from back rubs with wandering hands, to a peck on the lips, to a passionate make-out session in the backyard.

"Where'd you park?" Erinn asked as she pulled her face back.

We slipped out the gate, leaving the party behind, and walked hand in hand down the street. Loud voices faded into the distance, and only the sound of our footsteps hitting the pavement persisted.

"I hate Smart cars," I said as we passed by one on the street.

"That's my car," she said. "And it's fucking cute."

"Makes sense why we're going to mine," I laughed. "The old Toyota."

The Dethbox was no town car, but at least she had a back seat we could use. I opened the door for Erinn like a gentleman, then climbed in after.

"You look a little nervous," I said, positioning myself on top of her.

Erinn fumbled with the button on my jeans. "I've never, uh," she paused. "Like..."

"Never what?" I asked.

Her face flushed, and she pulled at her necklace. "Like, gone all the way before..."

I knew saving yourself for marriage was a Christian value, but I never imagined anyone lived by it, especially at this age. For a split second, I questioned the line.

"Do you still wanna do this?" I asked.

"Just cause I haven't, doesn't mean I don't want to."

My pants were down at that point, and my dick was throbbing in her hand. Lez had been more of a sport fuck, but that night with Erinn felt different. She was the type of girl I could see myself dating.

I was gentle at first, rubbing her clit before slipping a finger inside. She pulled at me, teasing, brushing the tip of my dick against her pussy until it was about to burst. Then I thrust inside her. She squinted, her lips parting slightly. I leaned in to kiss her as I pulled back slowly.

The Dethbox shook in rhythm with our movements, its old shocks groaning under the pressure as the chassis met the curb. Erinn wrapped her legs around me, forcing me deep inside her as she screamed in pleasure. I couldn't pull out in time, and I didn't want to either.

# Pulling Out

The next day, I met Backslash to drop off my weekly earnings. Mostly, it was just to report that I hadn't sold much since the rave. Dealing wasn't working out for me. A month of poor sales, capped off by last night's experience, really drove the point home.

Ecstasy was amazing, but I wasn't a dealer.

"What are you doing?" I asked, seeing that her laptop was open to Monster.com when I stepped into her bedroom.

"You're not making me any money," Backslash snapped.

"Sorry, I—"

"It's not you," she sighed. "I didn't grow up dreaming about selling drugs and fucking assholes like Miguel. I fell into this life because of who I knew and where I was. But all those people are gone, and I'm still here."

"Like your last dealer?" I asked, taking a seat on the bed next to her.

She turned away as a tear traced a dark path of liner down her face. Brushing the tear away, she smeared her makeup, then wiped her hand off on her black dress—the same black dress.

"I'm tired," she said after a minute.

"Me too," I admitted. "This doesn't feel like the life for me."

Backslash faced me, her gaze steady. I knew she wasn't surprised to hear that I wanted out. She'd been expecting this conversation, she'd planned for it, and she already had requirements in mind.

"My old dealer, Jenna," Backslash said. "She *was* my best friend."

"Was?"

"You suck at dealing," she said bluntly. "And I need cash now, so here's what's gonna happen. This dickhole Fate is gonna buy the rest of the pills at five dollars per." She paused, studying me. "I bet you're asking yourself why I'm being so cool about all this, right? Why am I being so fucking cool, Graves?"

"I dunno," I said, humoring her. "Why are you being so fucking cool, Slash?"

"Gee, I thought you'd never ask," she said, leaning in. "You're gonna figure out what happened to my best friend, because I haven't seen her since she started driving for Fate."

Drugs didn't give me much tension anymore, but selling a few hundred pills to a guy named Fate so I could investigate the case of a missing girl was sketch as fuck.

"Why don't you just call her?"

"Don't you think I've tried?" Backslash's gaze was fixed inward. With a sudden burst of energy, she hopped off the bed and paced. "She doesn't answer calls or respond to texts."

"Why?"

"She got weird the second she went there. Those people aren't like us, Graves... I just, I want to know that she's alive."

Watching Backslash pace around the room was unsettling. It was nice to hear her talk like we were on the same level, though. She always felt so far beyond me. But she was a different person that day. She was vulnerable, human.

"How dangerous is this guy?" I asked.

Backslash rolled her eyes. "Forget it," she said, snatching her purse off the dresser.

"I'll go there. I just wanna know what I'm getting into first."

"It wasn't fair of me to ask," she said. "Just keep selling the pills you have, and you'll be done when you're done. I'll have a new job by then too. And we can just forget about this mistake."

I got out of bed and gave her a hug, which felt as awkward as it sounded. She was not okay though, and she let me hold her. When I tightened my grip, she tightened hers too. There was a moment of quiet, and then she broke down.

"Don't worry," I said, as she sobbed into my shoulder. "I got this."

We sat on the bed together and talked about Jenna. She had bleached blonde hair and a Bowser tattoo on her arm. If those things weren't dead giveaways, she also wore a friendship bracelet Backslash had given her as a gift. All I had to do was sell the pills, find the girl, and report back.

# Fate's Apartment

Fate's door opened, releasing a peculiar odor. I couldn't help but sniff the air. It smelled like unwashed socks, but with sweet undertones. Gross, but alluring at the same time, like the aftermath of disaster.

The lean, pale dude who opened the door was confused by my sniffing.

"What's your problem?" he asked, pulling me inside.

People were sitting in a circle on the beige carpet. They all got quiet when I stumbled in, and they stared at me, sizing me up. Notebooks filled with odd geometric sketches lay beside the tense-looking crowd, along with Q-tips, several bobby pins, and a lighter.

"Which one of you is Fate?" I asked.

The guy who opened the door raised his hand. "Who the fuck else?"

After Backslash's breakdown, I'd imagined Fate as a hard ass with a fuse shorter than the pinky nail he used to snort coke. Kind of how I imagined Backslash as an older man before I'd met her. Fate was tall, six something, and abrasive, but he lacked the physical strength and presence needed to inspire fear in me.

"The price is thirty-one thirty-five," I said, taking off the backpack I'd carried the pills over in. "Six hundred twenty-seven hits."

Fate stroked his bare chin. "Zack, count 'em," he snapped.

If anything, I would've expected Zack to be in charge. A chiseled physique, six-pack abs, and prominent veins made him look scarier than Fate. He wasn't someone I wanted to hand the pills to.

"I need the money first." I said.

"This fucking guy." Fate threw his arms up and stomped down the hall. His actions were sudden and jerky, as if a feral animal were at the helm. "Give Zack the damn pills. I'll be back."

I reluctantly handed over the pills while the rest of the circle continued to stare at me in silence. Meanwhile, I heard Fate arguing with a girl in his room. Her voice was familiar.

There were only two girls in the circle. One was Mexican with black hair, the other was white like Jenna but heavyset with brown hair.

Fate walked back in. "I've got three grand."

The hunt for Jenna would have to wait. Fate was a haggler.

"The price is not negotiable," I told him. "Thirty-one thirty-five."

"How many pills are we at?" he asked Zack.

Zack glanced up from the pills and shrugged. "You messed up my count."

"Fucking useless," Fate said, handing me the three grand.

Backslash warned me Fate would try to stiff us, and if it came down to it, then I should use that as a bargaining chip to help figure out where Jenna was.

"I'll give you the discount," I said. "But I need you to answer a question."

Lez appeared in the hallway right as I asked Fate about Jenna. I knew I recognized her voice. That chick was everywhere.

"Where've you been?" she asked, her eyes darting as she spoke.

"Been trying to sell off these pills."

"Forget about the pills," Lez said, offering me a pipe. "You gotta hit this shit."

The pipe was glass, with a spherical bowl covered in soot, and a small opening at the top. A thin tube extended from its center.

Fate stole the pipe from Lez before. "Did you burn my fucking bowl?"

He marched into the kitchen and opened a drawer. There was a 9mm pistol inside, among other random stuff. My heart stopped when he reached his hand in, but all he pulled out was a Magic Eraser.

"Don't burn my bowl," he said, handing me the freshly cleaned pipe.

There was a hardened substance inside the bowl—meth. I knew what meth was from the "Not Even Once" campaign. There were billboards on the highways, featuring a battered mom and her tweaked-out kid. And there was a new show called Breaking Bad. Long story short, meth was a drug you didn't fuck with.

Lez handed me her lighter, ironically decorated with a custom label.

**Not. Even. Once.**

"I'm fine," I said. "I'll stick to the fun stuff."

A grin overtook Lez's face. "You know those green guns are meth bombs."

"Meth bombs?"

Fate was thrilled with my incompetence. "Is this guy for real?"

"No one ever told him there were drugs in his drugs," Lez snickered.

The circle burst out laughing, their first hint of life. Then my gaze dropped to the pipe in my hand. All those billboards, warnings, and horror stories, they should've stopped me, but they didn't. I'd already crossed that line, hadn't I? I took pills loaded with meth, and the world didn't end.

Maybe meth wasn't the evil drug people made it out to be. I told myself that it was just another high, the same as any other night, but deep down I knew I was lying. The boundaries that once held me back were slipping away. I put the stem to my lips and flicked Lez's lighter.

"You gotta spin it," Lez said, rubbing her thumb and forefinger together.

As I spun the pipe, the melted liquid danced along the cooler sides of the glass bowl, creating a plume of white smoke.

I inhaled, bracing for a coughing fit, but the meth went down smooth. I took the pipe from my mouth and exhaled a dense cloud. There was an unusual weight to it. The smoke fell from my mouth instead of drifting.

"Put that shit out," Fate snapped. "Don't waste it."

Lez stole the pipe, spit on her own shirt, then wiped the glass bowl with it. The sound of sizzling spit filled the air as the remaining meth hardened.

"How do you like getting spun?" she asked.

A shiver shot down my spine. Then my skin ignited. A sudden flush spread from my face to my fingertips. Blood surged through my veins until my whole body vibrated with raw, restless energy.

"Holy shit," I sputtered. "This is amazing."

Lez's eyes lit up. "Right?"

"I don't get why people act like this shit is evil."

Fate chimed in. "The evil is inside you. This shit gets it going."

The crew didn't look so tense to me anymore. I was on their level now, and it was crazy. I was lucid, all-powerful, superhuman. Everything was humming, and I was so distracted by it that I didn't see Lez move in for a kiss—she bit my lip and shoved her hand down my pants.

A deep, crawling unease entered the high as the circle watched. The room seemed to shift as they leaned in. It wasn't disgust that I saw in their eyes. It was yearning. They wanted to watch. The atmosphere pressed in around me, thick and suffocating, as I reacted to Lez's touch.

"Remember when you fucked my throat?" she whispered.

The unease intensified, forcing me to pull away. "This doesn't feel right."

"Are you gonna stop me?"

Lez dropped to her knees and unbuttoned my jeans. There were bugs crawling inside my stomach when she pulled my dick out in front of everyone, but I didn't stop her. Meth was different from ecstasy. It turned me primal.

My heart pumped, and my dick was harder than it'd ever been. There was no turning back now. With the crew watching, I grabbed Lez's head and shoved my dick down her throat.

Then Zack walked up and pulled down his pants.

Lez grabbed his dick while I fucked her throat. There was a twinge of jealousy from the girl who Zack was sitting next to. But when I released Lez's head, she started sucking his dick anyway, with a trail of my pre-cum running down the side of her mouth.

Fate walked up next, proudly resting his dick on Lez's face before giving her a couple of light smacks with it.

I retreated into the background, still stroking myself, almost involuntarily.

Zack finished fast, leaving Lez's face dripping with cum. She let his load run down her cheek and lips as she crawled to me. Her saliva turned into a thick, hot, lube that made her mouth feel even better.

Fate finished on her from the side, gluing her eyes shut as she gagged on my cock.

The excitement got too intense to handle. I wrapped both hands around her head and came down her throat so hard she choked. My heart hammered against my ribcage, faster than it had ever beaten before.

I collapsed on the floor, lying still, until my pulse leveled out. Meanwhile, Lez took a shower and changed into some of Fate's extra clothing. The crew ended up sprawling out on the carpet next to me, like nothing had even happened.

I couldn't begin to explain what went down that night, why it went down, or how one thing led to another. But I stayed there on the floor until I passed out late in the morning, still thinking about it.

I woke up when the front door opened. The lights were still on, but the crew was asleep. My limbs were twitching and uncomfortable, and I felt agitated. I closed my eyes and pretended I was sleeping. I wasn't ready for an interaction.

But I peeked as a girl with bleached blonde hair walked past.

I sat up, pretending she had woken me. "Hey," I whispered. "Jenna?"

"What of it?"

"I know your friend, Backslash."

Jenna spotted a bag of powder in the kitchen. "Is this coke fair game?"

"Wasn't there earlier," I said, meeting her at the counter.

Jenna emptied the powder onto the counter, grabbed a card from her wallet, and cut a line. I watched her longingly, my muscles tight. With a derisive glance in my direction, she cut a second smaller line.

"Backslash sent you to spy?" she asked.

I glanced at the friendship bracelet on her wrist. "She just wants to know that you're okay," I told her.

Jenna looked deep in thought. "It's been a while."

"You should call her."

"So she can yell at me?" Jenna's tone sharpened. "Backslash thinks she's better than us because she only messes with ecstasy. She says we're all creeps, and I don't know what I'm doing. Like, I know what I'm doing, bitch. These are my friends, so shut your fucking face."

"She's just worried about you," I said, and I couldn't help thinking about Levi, and how we'd left things.

"We grew up together," Jenna said. "She got me into drugs when her parents died. I spent every day with her, trying to make her feel better. Now she talks down to me and judges me."

"We doin' these lines?" I asked, growing impatient.

Jenna stuck a twenty in her nose and inhaled her line. Her eyes watered as she stared at me. She tried to speak, but her breath caught in her throat. Then a haunted look filled her eyes and her neck tightened. She dropped like a rock. Her head smacked the counter, and her eyes closed.

I pulled her eyelids apart. Her pupils were pinpoints. "Jenna!" I slapped her face. Her lips were turning blue. "Wake up," I shouted. "Help me," I screamed for the crew. "I need help here!"

Fate stumbled in, rubbing the sleep from his eyes. He took one look at Jenna and woke right up. His face turned as pale as the power Jenna just snorted.

"Not here," he said, pacing.

"She's dying."

"Not here," Fate repeated. "This fucking bitch cannot die here."

Lez and the crew had woken up and crowded around the kitchen. No one spoke. They just stared helplessly as a blue tint spread across Jenna's skin, becoming more pronounced by the second.

Fate turned his attention to the counter. "Who's fucking heroin is this?"

The crew remained tight-lipped. I didn't know they used heroin, or coke, or any of that shit, but I guess it shouldn't have come as a surprise.

"Jenna doesn't do H," Fate spat. "Who gave it to her?"

"That bitch was stealing." Lez said. "I dunno whose shit is on the counter, but if she took it without asking, that's on her."

Fate dragged his hands down his face. "We just need to fix this."

"I'll call 911," I said.

"Fuck no, you won't," he spat. "They can't come here."

I took my phone out anyway and moved away from the commotion. Behind me, I heard the kitchen drawer open. Steel scraped against steel as Fate racked the slide of his pistol and chambered a round. By the time he told me to "stop," I'd already dropped the phone.

"No one is calling anyone," Fate said. "You're not gonna run back to Backslash either, not 'til I know I can trust you."

I turned to face him. "Can't we at least take her to the hospital?"

Fate looked down at Jenna and sighed. "She's already dead. We need to get rid of her."

# State Route 85

Fate was squeezed in the back of the Dethbox with Zack and his girlfriend Ash, the Mexican chick from the circle. I learned the two were dating while we were wrapping Jenna's body in Fate's old bed sheets—her dead fucking body.

Lez sat up front with me, acting like nothing happened as we drove an hour to Buckeye on State Route 85.

"I said turn here." Fate smacked me from behind.

"There's no turn in."

"It's a fucking landfill, Graves. There's no paved roads."

The Dethbox shuddered as I jerked the wheel, trading asphalt for the jarring bumps of the landfill. Ahead, the terrain got worse. The car shook violently, its tires bouncing over deep ruts and grooves left by the trucks, and every time the shocks bumped Jenna's body smacked the top of the trunk.

"Stop there," Fate said.

I hit the brakes and killed the engine.

The smell of rotting trash assaulted my nostrils. It was a sharp smell, burnt urine and rotten eggs. The decay made my stomach churn, and the idea of burying Jenna in the garbage added to the nausea.

"Come on, Graves." Fate slapped the trunk. "Sun's coming up."

I threw my door open and popped the trunk. Jenna's body, only half covered by the thin sheet we'd wrapped her in, felt cold to the touch. Her face was exposed. I couldn't stop staring at it.

Fate showed no regard when he grabbed her shoulder and yanked her body from the trunk. "Get her feet," he said, stumbling back.

I shut my eyes, gripped Jenna's ankles, and helped lay her down next to the Dethbox. Meanwhile, Lez, Zack, and Ash dug a pit in the trash pile with their bare hands. Fate assured us the body would stay hidden. Every day a trash delivery came, and every day, that trash was covered in a fresh layer of dirt.

Once the hole was dug, Fate and I tossed Jenna into it. The fact that she died after one little mistake didn't make sense. She was so undeserving of this ending, I couldn't handle it.

My hands trembled as I prayed on my crucifix. I didn't know if anyone was listening, but I hoped they were. Before we covered her in the trash, I knelt down and snuck Backslash's friendship bracelet off her wrist.

"It's not too late," I said. "We can take her somewhere else."

Fate dusted off his hands. "The bitch doesn't care where she's buried."

These were her so-called friends, the people she was defending moments before her death. The people she sacrificed a genuine friendship with Backslash for. They threw her in the fucking trash. Backslash wasn't perfect, but she was right, these people weren't like us.

We finished covering Jenna as the sun crested the mountains. Then, everyone jumped in the Dethbox and we drove away, leaving Jenna to rot. The entire drive home I wondered what I was going to tell Backslash about her friend, and how I could ever live with this secret.

Backslash was waiting outside Fate's apartment when we returned. The sun was out, already blazing hot, but a chill ran down my spine. Her gaze was locked on mine.

Fate and Lez talked shit about her as we walked up, while Zack and Ash followed behind, keeping to themselves.

Backslash stepped in front of me. "Where were you?"

Lez turned as she walked around me. "Have fun with that crazy bitch."

"Go suck a dick, ho," Backslash snapped.

Fate strode past, showing me the pistol in his waistband. He opened the door, letting Lez, Zack, and Ash inside. Then he turned back and glared at me, a silent threat in his eyes as he stepped through the door.

Backslash crossed her arms. "When I call, you answer."

"Relax, I got your money."

"Answer your fucking phone next time." Backslash punched my shoulder.

My whole body was buzzing, and not in a good way. With everything going on, I forgot I even had a phone, not that it should've mattered. There was no deadline when I left, and I never reported back to her right after a deal.

Lez leaned out of the apartment. "You coming or what, Graves?"

"One sec," I said.

"You two are friends now?" Backslash asked.

"I met Lez a while ago. I didn't know you two knew each other."

"I know everyone. That's why I warned you about them," she said. "Whatever. Did you learn anything about Jenna from Fate and that fucking ho-bag or was this totally pointless?"

I couldn't stop picturing Jenna snorting that line, the look of death on her face, or her clammy skin. I could still smell the trash we buried her in. Backslash must smell it too. It was on me.

"Well?" Backslash asked, keeping the pressure on.

"I talked to Jenna," I admitted. But that was all I could say. If I told her what happened, then Fate would take me out, or I'd get arrested, so I told a partial truth. "Jenna doesn't want to see you."

"You're lying."

I closed my eyes, reached in my pocket, and pulled out the friendship bracelet. "She said loves you very much, but..." I fumbled for words. "She's not the person you knew before, and she's sorry."

Backslash took the bracelet, and before she could ask me anything else, I handed her the cash. She licked her finger and counted out the bills, but her eye contact never wavered.

"This is only three grand."

"We talked about that. You knew he was—"

"Forget it." Backslash pocketed the cash. "Forget about your cut, too."

"But I owe Damien rent."

Backslash shrugged. "I don't do business with liars, and you're a fucking liar, Graves."

She didn't know what the truth was, only that I was lying. Then she paused, seeming to wait for my confession, like she knew I was about to break, but I kept my mouth shut until she gave up. Things had gone too far. I needed to get a job, pay Damien, and take my life back.

# Opportunity

Damien fixed the Velcro on his tan and maroon shoes, lined up his shot, then strode up the lane. His bowling ball flirted with the gutter before hanging a sharp left and smashing into the pocket.

The clatter of pins did nothing but add to my pounding headache. I was sure Damien brought me there just to mess with me.

"See that shit?" he asked with a proud look in his eyes.

"Sure did, hole in one."

"Come on, man." Damien took his seat. "You know damn well it's a strike."

Aside from the smell of chicken nuggets and fries, the bowling alley held no appeal. Between the noise, my aching muscles, and general exhaustion, hurling a fifteen-pound ball was the last thing I wanted to do.

"I never pictured you as a bowler," I said.

"Look man, drugs are fine, but there's more to life. I do it all because getting hung up on one thing ain't good. Life is about balance and experience. Now get up there and roll your damn shot."

Lifting the ball pulled my fingers from their sockets. A hollow rushing sound filled my head as my vision blacked over. If it weren't for the fan on the ball return, I would've passed out right there. After my vision returned, I stumbled across the polished wood and flung the ball straight into the gutter.

"You went in too hard," Damien said.

I collapsed next to him. "The ball is heavy."

"The ball ain't the problem," he said, turning to face me. "It's the drugs."

Damien rolled another strike, and an alien spaceship flickered onto the tube display above the lane. It cast a green tractor beam and abducted ten poorly animated pins from a field.

"They haven't updated that shit since the '90s," I said, changing the subject.

Damien asked me point blank. "You got the rent, brother?"

It wasn't like I could land a job that day. The only way I could pay Damien was with my cut of the ecstasy, which I would've taken ahead of time if I knew Backslash was going to turn on me.

"If you can smooth things over with Slash, I'll have the rent."

"That's all you, man."

I brushed past Damien, grabbed a ball off the return, and flung it down the lane. I went back to my seat without looking, but I heard the ball make contact right as Lez buzzed my phone.

> Since u fucked up ur gig with Backslash, I talked to Fate (ur welcome). You've got a car, and experience, and Jenna won't be driving anymore… There's a score goin down later.

What kinda score?

> A big one, and there's no one else we can trust with a car right now.

I need to make a couple hundred.

Whatever, we can work something out.

Damien leaned over my shoulder. "You ain't learned your lesson yet?"

I think I got the point. Lez was nuts, but a couple hundred would cover the rent, and keep a roof over my head so I could figure things out. And if we're being honest, that was all an excuse. Because my entire body was breaking down, and what I really needed was meth.

I'm in.

Awesome, I'll let Fate know.

Just to be clear, I'm not your new driver. I'm in for one score, a hit of the pipe, and however much money Fate can pay me.

# The Score

Lez checked her MapQuest printout. "Turn in there."

Six guys were sitting on top of a gold Cadillac, its chassis sunk into the ground. They'd been laughing and passing a bottle around when we turned in, but they went straight-faced as we drove by.

"That wasn't them, right?" I asked as a guy hopped off the hood.

The next thing I knew, their bottle shattered on our back windshield. I stepped on the gas, putting some distance between us.

"Relax," Lez said. "They're not gonna follow."

"I don't like this place."

"It's gonna be fine," she assured me. "Pull over there."

As soon as we stopped, three guys emerged from the tear-down across the street. There was a gaunt white dude with sunken eyes and pale skin, and two black dudes who towered over him. I didn't get junkie vibes from them. They were hired muscle.

As the trio neared the Dethbox, the gaunt dude and Lez exchanged nods.

"Thought you never met these guys," I said.

Lez looked over at me. "I haven't... just being friendly," she said. "Fate set up the deal. The tweaker is Skel, obviously. He told me the big guys are Jamal and Murphy."

"Which one's which?"

Skel knocked on the window. “Everybody out.”

I didn’t want to get out. Backslash never would’ve done it like that. We could easily be beaten, robbed, or left for dead. But Lez hopped right out, so I cut the engine and got out too.

“Keys,” Skel demanded, like I was going to hand over the Dethbox.

“Where’s the stuff?” I asked.

Jamal and Murphy took defensive stances around Skel as he spoke. “I don’t shit where I eat,” he said. “There’s a drop house a few hoods down. Imma drive us there, you can’t know.”

“Can’t know what?”

“Where it is, man.” Skel was getting pissed. “Give me the fucking keys.”

With thousands of dollars of meth on the line, not to mention our lives, negotiation wasn’t an option. I handed Skel the keys. Lez rode in the front seat, while I got sandwiched in the back between Jamal and Murphy.

“Heads down,” Skel ordered.

Jamal forced my head onto the console, or maybe it was Murphy, who knows?

Skel directed Lez to his crotch. “Your head goes here, bitch.”

Lez gave him the finger and put her head on the dash. Then Skel sped off, grinding the Dethbox’s gears like he’d never driven a stick. Every shift jolted my poor car and slammed my head into the center console. By the time we screeched to a stop, I was about ready to faint.

“That wasn’t so bad,” Skel said as we got out. “Now give me the money.”

Lez obeyed, handing over the cash, just like that.

What the fuck kind of operation was Fate running? I lit a cigarette and drew the smoke deep into my lungs as Skel ordered Jamal and Murphy to run in and get the crystal from their stash house.

I smoked my cigarette to the filter waiting.

"What's taking them so long?" I asked, flicking the butt into the street.

Skel shrugged.

"Well find out," Lez said. "We need to get going."

Skel nodded and vanished into the house, just like Jamal and Murphy had. And just like Jamal and Murphy, he didn't come back. The realization struck me and Lez at the same time—Skel had the money.

We burst into the house and were met with the echoing silence of an empty room. The carpet had vacuum lines on it, and the air smelled like wet paint. It wasn't a drop house. The place was for sale. The back door was wide open, and there was no trace of Jamal, Murphy, or Skel.

"They're fucking gone, Lez," I shouted. "Fuck!"

"Why are you yelling at me?"

"Because you gave them our cash without seeing the fucking drugs. They walked right through the house and left us here with nothing."

"That's not my fault," she shot back. "You didn't stop them."

"How could I have stopped them?" I asked. "The only way to make sure people don't rip you off is to not trust them. Those were clearly not trustworthy people. Seriously, are you fucking dumb?"

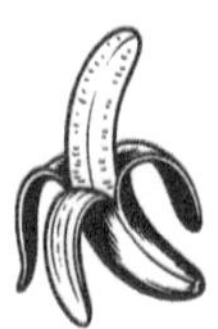

The drive back to Fate's was filled with an uncomfortable silence, until Lez unfolded a piece of crumpled aluminum foil, making sure not to rip the delicate metal. A tiny ball of black gunk clung to the center of the foil.

"Black tar," she said. "It'll help you calm down."

"No thanks," I said, clutching the wheel. "I needed the meth."

Lez shrugged, put a straw in her mouth, and heated the foil with her lighter. A pungent, burnt-plastic odor filled the Dethbox. After what had happened to Jenna, I hated heroin, but it must've made Lez immune to giving a fuck, because she was passed out by the time we got to Fate's apartment.

"Wake up," I said, giving her shoulder a shake. "I need you for this."

Lez opened one bloodshot eye, muttered something incomprehensible, then laid her head back on the seat.

I shook her harder. "Seriously, what do we say?"

"Don't worry," she murmured, her eyes still sealed shut. "I have a plan."

Her plan needed to be immaculate, but as she hung on my shoulder, stumbling over the pavement, I had my doubts. Seriously, why did anyone do heroin? I liked being awake and aware, and I hated not being able to talk to Lez like a human being. The crew's eyes were on us the second we stepped inside, and it didn't take them long to realize we came back empty.

Fate walked out of his room. "Well," he asked. "Where is it?"

"You sent us into a—"

"Those guys," Lez cut in, stumbling over her words. "Like, stole our cash."

The vein in Fate's neck bulged, like a thick, blue rope beneath his skin. He went to the kitchen, opened the drawer, and took his pistol out. "You think you can rip me off?" he asked.

"It's not like that," I said.

Fate kept his finger on the trigger. "Give me your wallet."

"There's nothing in it, but sure," I said, tossing him my empty wallet.

He kept the gun was pointed at my head, using his left hand to search the wallet. The gun shook every time he twitched. I pressed my eyes shut. I couldn't look at his finger, which was sliding over the trigger. Finally, he put the gun down, took my license, and snapped a pic.

"I know where you fucking live, Graves."

"Well, I moved."

"Then why are you scared?" he asked. "Who lives there, your mommy?"

"My mom's dead, and I'm shaking because you have a gun pointed at me and I haven't smoked any fucking meth. If I robbed you, do you think I'd be coming back here afterwards?"

"Someone you care about lives there. I can smell it on you."

"Oh my God, he didn't jack you," Lez said.

She was standing up on her own now. Her speech was clearer. It must have been the adrenaline. She strutted up to Fate and started playing with his collar.

"I think I know how to fix this," she said.

"Seriously?" I asked her. "That was your big plan?"

Lez winked over her shoulder, then disappeared down the hall with Fate, leaving me with the crew. Zack must've sensed my frustration because he handed me a pipe and lighter.

I took a seat in the circle, hit the pipe, and let the meth work its magic.

"What's your name?" I asked, handing the pipe to the only other guy in the crew.

"Angel," he said with a flamboyant grin.

"Is Lez in there doing what I think she's doing?" I asked.

A slow smile stretched across Angel's face as a series of retching and gagging cries answered my question.

"Oh honey, she's really goin' for it," he said. "You don't like-like her, do you?"

He handed the pipe back to me, instead of passing it to Sam, the girl next to him, and I swear she looked like she wanted to kill him for it. I took a small hit and passed it to her next.

"Well, do you like Lez?" she asked.

Lez was kind of a slut. But meth supercharges emotions. I felt jealous, even though I shouldn't've. And I liked her, even though Fate's dick was down her throat.

Ash snapped her fingers in front of Sam's face. "Pass the pipe, ho."

It took a minute for me to realize I never responded to Sam, and by that time Lez was walking down the hall with a cum stained shirt, dragging a satisfied Fate behind her. My stomach was on fire, my chest was tight, and my dick was rock hard.

Fucking meth. That shit was like Viagra on steroids.

Lez sat next to me, radiating warmth. She was still out of breath, and her nipples were poking through her shirt. Sucking him off must have woken her all the way up because she was speaking loud and clear.

"You cost Fate a lot of money," she said.

"You were holding the cash," I said. "I never would've paid first."

"Doesn't matter." Lez breathed heavily into my ear as she ran her hand over the bulge in my pants. "I have a plan for you."

"What are you talking about?"

"You don't have to worry about rent, 'cause you're gonna live with me. Fate needs a new driver, so instead of having to pay him back, you're gonna earn the money back by driving us."

"I told you I wasn't your driver."

Fate spoke up, his voice stern. "That's your only play."

"How do you pay your rent?" I asked Lez.

"My dad is loaded," she said. "He ditched my mom, so guilt pays for my apartment."

"Rich fuck," Fate scoffed.

"Can you just pay Fate back and I'll owe you instead?" I asked. "This wasn't my fault."

"My dad and I don't really talk. He lives in another state and pays the rent straight to the complex. Everything else is on me.

You're gonna love it though. I live in Scottsdale and it's fucking tits."

# SCOTTSDALE

Lez's place *was* fucking tits. It had a vaulted ceiling and a fireplace, not that you need fire in Arizona. And there were bitches in Juicy Couture pants walking French bulldogs around the property. I felt bad, kind of. Those orange-tanned blondes had no idea there was a cancer growing in their midst.

The perfectly manicured landscape reminded me of the park Sadie and I used to play at. Oh shit, Sadie. I had less than a year to get my shit together, and I was in deeper than ever.

"Stop staring out the window," Lez said.

I closed the blinds and joined her on the couch, sinking into the plush cushions.

"I have to admit, your bed is amazing. I slept great."

Lez grabbed a small purse from the counter and sat next to me. "Wanna spin a bowl?"

"I shouldn't."

"Okay," she said, rolling her eyes.

"I need to make money," I told her. "Not use the shit we're gonna sell."

Lez unpacked her purse on the coffee table in front of us. There was a meth pipe named Spin-derella, some bobby pins, and a straw. Not a normal straw though, one she'd cut short and at an angle. Its tip was slanted like a tiny spade.

"You're having a blinding moment of clarity," she explained, as she used the straw to scoop shards from a dime bag and drop them into Spin-derella. "People get these moments, you know. And they throw away their pipes and they think they're gonna change their life and shit, but they never do."

"I have to. I have a kid."

Lez laughed, "No, you don't."

"I do."

"If you did, you wouldn't be here. You're a tweaker."

"I'm not a tweaker."

"Whatever you say." Lez melted the crystal, cooled the bowl, then blew the smoke out of it. "Never smoke the first melt," she said. "It's nasty."

"I don't think you're hearing me. Remember when you told me your ex, Ryder, knocked up some other bitch while you two were dating? Well, I was dating the other bitch, Eva."

Lez looked me in the eye and laughed. "That's why you were acting so weird."

"Eva's my ex, and Sadie is my kid."

For the first time, a flicker of sympathy played on Lez's face. "Sadie... she isn't yours."

"Ryder's the one living with her, but I'm her dad."

"No, you're not."

Lez pulled out her phone and showed me a message from Ryder.

Eva's having my baby, so I'm all in.

I never considered the the possibility that I was raising someone else's kid. But I checked the date on the message, and everything lined up.

"Blinding moments," Lez said, handing me the pipe. "They never last."

My blinding moment had just been shattered. Without Sadie, there was no reason for me to change. I held the flame under the bowl, watching the crystal melt into a shimmering, viscous pool as the sweet smell of smoke filled the air. Then I held the pipe to my lips, spun it, and inhaled.

The pain couldn't reach me, not if I kept myself high.

"It's alright," Lez said. "You've got a job, and a place. I'm here for you."

I coughed out a cloud of smoke. "Are you?" I asked. "What are we even? What the fuck is this? Like I live with you, but you're just choking yourself out on everyone's dicks?"

"Fate needed a driver. You needed a free spot."

"Well, we're hooking up and now I live with you, and you treat me like I'm more than a friend."

Lez shrugged.

"'Cause if we're gonna be together, you can't just, like, fuck everyone."

"I'm not fucking anyone," Lez snatched the pipe and took a hit, then started talking at me as she blew out the smoke. "Blowjobs are like currency. That's just how you get shit done."

"What about blowbangs?"

Lez laughed. "That was sperm of the moment."

"Great, you're fucking hilarious. So, we live together but we're not dating and blowjobs are currency with an unclear exchange rate?"

"If it's that important to you, then ask me the fuck out."

"Wanna go out?"

She shrugged. "I guess."

"You're not allowed to fuck anyone else," I told her. "That's where I draw the line."

"Fine."

"Great. Then, that's the fucking plan."

Using a straightened bobby pin, Lez scraped the white residue from the pipe stem into the bowl. "Let's save the shards for later," she said, acting like we hadn't argued at all. "You can take this hit, though. You need it." She smiled and offered me the pipe. "The scrape burns fast, so no waiting for it to melt or it's gonna vanish. You need to hit it as soon as you light it."

She was like a drug Yoda. If Yoda were a cumslut.

Too bad she wasn't more like Erinn. I could date a girl like Erinn. This was just fucking confusing. I lit the scrape and breathed deep, but it did little to lift my mood. My whole life had been built on a lie.

"So," I said, daring to reflect on the absurdity that was my life. "I've been raising someone else's kid, and now she's gone..."

"Don't look at this like it's a bad thing." Lez took the pipe from me and packed it away in her drug purse. "Things are gonna be fun here, and there's no one you need to worry about."

"No one at all."

Life *was* simpler before Sadie—uninhibited. I'd been a peacemaker who never argued with anyone, and I hated fighting with Eva. If this was my life for the foreseeable future, why not surrender to it? Why not have fun? It'd be an adjustment, but I could learn how to be happy.

# A Few Weeks Later... I Think

I spent hours picking at my skin, searching the carpet for lost shards. The world shrank to a blur of blood, fibers, and need. That's what rock bottom looks like: desperation, dizziness, and solitude.

My body was rejecting the drug in glorious fashion. There was a shard of meth poking out of my arm. And I thought, if only I could grab it, I could smoke it again. I clenched my left fist, pinching the shard with a pair of tweezers, and pulled. The shard broke free, leaving a small, stinging hole in my flesh.

"Lez, bring the pipe."

"Graves," Lez yelled. "I swear to God, if you're picking your arm."

"I'm not."

Lez walked in, arms crossed. "Seriously?"

"Whatever," I said, holding up the tweezers. "Let's fucking smoke."

Lez snatched the tweezers from me. "Smoke what?"

The crystal fell, vanishing into the maze of carpet fibers below. I was really starting to resent that bitch. I don't know how long we'd been doing this. Time had lost its meaning, but it was too long.

"When's the last time you slept?" she asked.

"Sorry that I'm not passed out on heroin every minute of every fucking day."

Lez chewed her tongue, her face twisted, but she said nothing. What happened to the rave girl I met? It felt like her entire personality was derivative of whatever drug she was on at the time, and heroin was the cunt-iest of all.

"Nobody likes a carpet surfer," she said, throwing the pipe at me.

I shot her a dirty look. "It's not carpet surfing if it's my own shit. If I were searching on Fate's floor, that would be carpet surfing. I pulled this shard out of my body. It belongs to me."

"You're delusional."

A bright red trail of blood ran down my arm. I must've gone in harder than I realized. But the blood trail revealed something I'd missed before: tiny changes in flow, more shards.

"You need to stop," Lez said. "Seriously, go to bed."

I dropped a newly sourced shard into Spin-derella and dug back into my arm. Within a few minutes the pipe was loaded, and I lit it up.

"Why isn't there smoke?" I asked, investigating the bowl.

"Because you haven't slept and you're fucking delusional!"

"What do we do now?"

"Skim shards off your next deal," she said with a shrug. "Borrow money, or steal shit, whatever."

"That's stupid."

"Call someone then, I dunno. I can only suck so much dick, and it doesn't make extra meth appear when there's not enough to go around. If you want more right now, you're gonna have to pay Fate."

Cash had become rarer than meth. I pulled my phone out and started clicking through the contacts. I couldn't borrow from Levi. He'd been blowing up my phone, and I'd been ignoring him. Backslash was out for obvious reasons. I buried her best friend. And I straight bailed on Damien and never paid rent, so he was out. And all my other friends I lost touch with after becoming a father.

Then I saw Erinn's name, and a smile crossed my face.

Lez craned her neck. "Who's she?"

"This girl who would totally buy some shit, I'll have her meet us at Fate's."

Without thinking it through, I called Erinn. Despite nutting in her and never calling her back, and despite my current girlfriend hovering over me like she was going to murder me. I shouldn't have called. I knew better. But I needed meth. It was the only thing I could think about.

# The Call

## Erinn

Erinn rotated the click-wheel on her iPod, turning down "Pretty Handsome Awkward," so she could answer the phone. But when she pulled her phone from her jean pocket, and saw who was calling, she froze.

"Chels!" she yelled for her roommate.

A moment later, Chels appeared in the doorway. "You alright?"

"It's him."

Chels shifted, crossing her arms. "Who?"

Erinn jumped out of her bed and showed Chels her phone.

**Graves <3**

Chels' face fell. Her lips twisted into a sneer. The call ended, and the phone screen faded to black.

"What do I do?"

"Give me the phone," Chels demanded. "I'm deleting his number."

Erinn shoved the phone in her pocket. "Yeah, yeah, I know."

"You obviously don't know. Delete that rapist from your phone. Now."

"It wasn't like that."

Chels tapped her foot, and Erinn could hear how pissed off she was. "You went to that party a virgin. You didn't want to hook up. Then he dosed you, and then he fucked you."

Erinn's tone sharpened. "I asked for the drugs."

"You had no idea what you were asking for," Chels said. "He did."

Erinn jumped when her phone buzzed again. She looked at the light shining from her pocket. *Why did I ask Chels to come in*, she wondered. *To stop me?*

Chels would never forgive her for answering Graves, but when Erinn thought about it, she needed to talk to him. She had questions. Like where had he been? Why hadn't he called, and why was he calling now?

"Hey," she answered, waving Chels away.

Chels threw up her arms and stormed out. "Fuck you, rape guy."

"Who was that?" Graves asked. His voice sounded frantic.

"Are you okay?"

Graves hesitated, then said, "Fine. We should hang out."

Erinn walked to her vanity, twirling a strand of hair. "Totally, when?"

"Tonight."

Erinn looked at the clock on the counter. "It's like eleven o'clock already."

"Fuck, uh, tomorrow then. Bring twenty bucks."

"Twenty bucks..." she paused.

"Yeah, there's this thing you really gotta try, but I'm short on cash. It'll be lots of fun, promise. I'll text you the address."

"Okay," Erinn said, her voice shaking. Then, after a minute, she added, "I'd like to talk about what happened between us. We shared something special, and you went dark on me."

"Sure, talk soon."

The line went dead, and Erinn sat down on the bed. Graves didn't sound like the same fun guy she'd met at the party. She wondered if the person she met was a symptom of the drugs, and if he even liked her, or cared about what they'd shared. She thought they worked well together. In fact, the party had been replaying in her mind every night for the past couple of months.

Erinn pulled into a run-down apartment complex. Rust stains streaked the off-white walls, and there were a ton of beaters in the lot. She parked, made sure her door was locked, and hurried to the building.

A tall, skinny guy answered. "Who the fuck are you?"

"Ugh, sorry!" she said, pinching her nose. "I have the wrong place."

The guy grabbed her shirt and pulled her inside, then slammed the door shut behind her. The small apartment was filled with people sitting on the floor in a circle. They looked wrecked. Sunken, bloodshot eyes, disheveled hair, and a smell that said they hadn't bathed or changed their clothes in weeks.

"Who are you?" the skinny guy demanded.

"Erinn," she stammered, looking down.

"I'm Fate," he said. "Why the fuck are you knocking on my door?"

"I was looking for my friend Graves."

"No shit," Fate said. "Well, you're in luck, Graves and Lez are on their way."

"Who's Lez?"

Fate laughed and walked away, leaving Erinn surrounded by a crew of silent strangers. She looked around for a place to wait. There was no couch, no chairs. There was nothing to sit on except the carpet.

A guy outside the circle was playing "Through the Fire and Flames" by DragonForce in Guitar Hero III on a TV pushed against the wall.

"Cool song," Erinn said, taking a seat next to him.

Watching the game meant she didn't have to socialize. Her eyes stayed fixed on the screen, her legs were crossed, and her hands rested between them. Nobody bothered her. Even so, she hoped Graves would show up soon to help ease the tension.

# Another First

Graves

When I got to Fate's, Erinn was sitting in the corner. Her face lit up when she locked eyes with me, but her smile faded the second she noticed Lez. She realized I hadn't called her to hook up I guess.

"Sorry we're late," I said. "The 101 was closed."

Erinn got up, wiping off her pants like she had been sitting in dirt. "It's fine."

"Did you bring the money?"

"I should go, actually." She brushed past me, headed for the door.

I ran after her, trying to steady my hands as I caught her shoulder. Even my voice shook when I begged her to stay. "Then we can talk," I promised her. "Just stay here and chill, okay?"

She peered over my shoulder, her gaze on Lez. That's when I noticed her lips trembling and her eyes watering. Was she about to cry?

I should've been sympathetic, but I was just annoyed. It was like I had the devil in me. A primal hunger gnawed at my flesh, like a darkness demanding to be fed. I couldn't really think about what she was feeling.

"You clearly don't care about talking to me," Erinn said.

"I mean, we only hooked up like—"

Lez stepped between me and Erinn. "I'll take that money now."

Instead of asserting herself as my girlfriend, Lez went straight to business. There was a tone in her voice, a quiet dominance, and Erinn handed over her cash without questioning it. I realized then I'd been given a pass.

"Is this like, a deal?" Erinn asked as Lez walked to Fate's bedroom.

"Yeah, but you're gonna love it," I promised her. "It's even better than ecstasy. You just bought a bowl, so now we can talk and stuff."

"Talking to you costs money?"

I sat down and asked her to join me. "This will help us say what we mean."

Erinn refused to sit. Her feet were pointed at the door. Her posture, stiff. She should've left before it was too late, but I asked her to stay, and she agreed. Some delusional fairy-tale was playing in the back of her mind, making her think that we could be more than just friends.

"Who's the girl?" she asked.

As if on cue, Lez came back with the meth, threw it in my lap, and then went back to Fate's room. That confirmed it. Lez was letting me pretend I was single, so we could call Erinn again if we needed.

"Lez is my, uh... roommate."

The crew was silent. They were interested to see how that clusterfuck would play out. I used the uncomfortable silence to load the pipe. My mind was consumed with hitting that shit and letting the smoke cleanse me, but I pushed those thoughts aside long enough to give Erinn the first hit.

"Hold the flame under the bowl," I told her.

She clutched the pipe. Everyone in the crew stared at her, waiting. It was customary for the buyer to take the first hit, but they usually didn't take so long. She looked like a sheep surrounded by hungry wolves, her breath slow and heavy.

"I dunno," she said. "You take it, then we'll talk."

"You're gonna love it."

I flipped my Zippo open and held the pipe to her lips. I knew it'd make her feel better. She'd be on our level, and we could talk the way we had before. The flame danced beneath the bowl as my hand worked the pipe.

Erinn exhaled her first hit and looked at me, trembling. "I don't like this."

"You will," I said.

With her turn out of the way, I took my hit. Amphetamine flooded my system. The dopamine surge cleansed my mind, eliminating the mental debris that clouded my thoughts and emotions.

Only then, with the devil sated, could I see what I'd done to Erinn. It was like the feeling of disgust that creeps up after you blow your load into your hand. Guilt and shame tainted the hit. I didn't know what to do with that awful feeling. Meth was supposed to make me better.

"I'm sorry I called you," I said, and I meant it.

I passed the pipe to an anxious-looking Angel and turned my attention back to Erinn. Her face and hands were twitching. Not normal twitches, spasms.

"You need to relax," I said. "You're gonna have a heart attack."

Lez walked down the hall with Fate. "Graves," she said. "You're going on a drop."

"I can't right now. Erinn's not feeling good."

Erinn jumped up, still shaking. "It's f...fine," she stammered. "I need to go."

"Jesus-fuck," Fate said, looking at her. "You cannot leave my place tweaking like that."

"I n...need to."

"Sit your ass down," Fate yelled. "The neighbors are always watching us. If you leave tweaking, they'll call the cops. You're staying, and Graves," he said, "you're dropping shit off."

# Three-Eyed John

The car in front of me had six-six-six on its license plate. Meth makes you paranoid, and even though I didn't know what I believed, I pressed on the brakes and put some distance between me and that bad omen.

It wasn't the first time I'd seen a plate like that while dealing. My mom would've said it was a sign that I was headed down the wrong road. That whatever was at the end of that road had plans for me, and I wasn't going to like them.

When I got to the address, I parked behind an old Harley with a Desert Vultures sticker on the back. I cut the engine and grabbed the meth from the glove box. It was a larger order than usual, which brought me back to what Lez had said about skimming some off the top. It felt better to rip off a tweaker than to use Erinn again.

I checked over my shoulder, opened the Ziploc bag, grabbed a few shards, and threw them in the glove box. Then I walked up to the porch. The door cracked open before I reached it.

"What do you want?" John asked.

"Brought your friend, Crystal," I said through the crack.

He slammed the door. Two locks turned, then a chain slid, but the door never opened. A minute later, I let myself in and found the foyer empty. I followed the sound of a TV down the dim hallway.

Fucking tweakers, man. I didn't like them.

Their houses were creepy, their rules were stupid, and nothing was ever consistent. I'd been on too many sketchy deals, sitting in the Dethbox in shit neighborhoods, meeting in back alleys, and it was wearing thin.

The first doorway I checked had a kid gaming in it. That was new. He was facing away from me, so I sneaked past. Who lets a random dealer wander their house with a kid inside?

"Took you long enough," John huffed when I got to his room.

He was turned away from me, fiddling with stuff on his dresser. There was an eyeball tattooed on the back of his bald head. That's when his name clicked—Three-Eyed John. What the fuck? His wife didn't look much better. Her flesh was bruised and hanging off her bones.

"You gettin' spun, hun?" she asked.

John turned to face me. "Sure he is. Nobody leaves here tired."

I looked past John and saw that he was calibrating a scale. In all the deals I'd run, no one ever weighed their shit before. Then again, no one ordered in ounces. I needed to get my ass out of there.

"I'm fine, thanks," I said. "Got a tight schedule today."

John grabbed the meth. He squinted as he slapped the cash into my hand. I must've offended him when I refused his Southern hospitality.

Without speaking a word, John brought the bag straight to his scale. I started backing up, but when I got to the edge of the room, he turned around.

"Stop," he said.

His wife hopped out of bed. "Is he fixin' to rip us off?"

"Course not," I said.

John held up the bag, flexing his tree trunk sized arm. "You're light."

"I weighed it myself," I lied. "Your scale is off."

"Scale's fine," John said.

"Bag weight then."

John's wife waved her finger. "You don't wanna mess with him, hun."

Her words were a clear threat, and a warning. She looked like she'd taken plenty of punches, and if John hit his own wife, who knew what he'd do to me. I tried to leave, but before I could take a step, John grabbed my arm and slammed me against the wall.

"I'm taking a hundred back," he said, wrapping his fingers around my neck.

"I... only took a couple," I choked.

"Oh." John let go. "Why didn't you say so?"

He drew back and slammed his fist into my face. The world went dark for a second. A sharp ring pierced my ears as my body was hurled across the floor. It wasn't like getting punched by Ryder. That shit knocked me into the next day. I barely registered his wife rifling through my pockets until she pulled out a hundred. And before I knew it, John had me pinned against the wall again.

His wife cast a worried look at the door. "Little Johnny's gonna hear you."

"So what?" John snarled.

"We got the money back," she said. "Now let him go."

Whatever adrenaline surge took control of John's body, it dissipated, and he dropped me to my feet. I stole a look at the scale, and the weight was way off. A lot more than the few small shards I took could account for, which meant Fate was already shorting people, with my safety on the line.

"I didn't realize it was like that," I said.

"You tried to take something from me," John said, tearing the crucifix off my neck. "It's only fair I take something from you."

John's wife slapped his shoulder. "What would Jesus think?"

"Who gives a crap?" John asked. "Our friend here needs to learn a lesson. Something important. He's gonna remember this night."

"You can't steal Jesus," she snorted. "It just ain't right."

John shook his head, mumbling, "This woman'll be the death of me," under his breath as he threw the crucifix at me. "Get out of my sight, kid. Before I change my goddamn mind."

I was about to return to Fate's even deeper in debt. It was Fate's fault, but my problem. A misunderstanding about bag weight could've explained the amount I'd taken, but Fate, that motherfucker, he sent me there short.

In any case, John had given me more than a bloody nose and a concussion. He gave me an idea. The crucifix had lost its meaning. I didn't need it anymore. But I could bring it to the pawnshop down the road and return to Fate with the full amount and the stolen shards.

# God's Girl

## Erinn

Erinn repositioned herself. Sensation returned to her leg, causing a tingle. Fate and Lez were in the bedroom together, and the crew had been ordered to make sure she didn't leave.

Her gut screamed at her, "Run!," but she stayed put.

"Love your necklace, honey," Angel smiled at Erinn. It was the first thing anyone had really said to her.

"Just what we needed," Sam said. "Another skinny bitch."

"Meth makes everyone skinny," Angel said.

Sam pulled her shirt up, letting her stomach out over her pants. "Not everyone."

"Oh, honey," Angel patted Sam's head. "Literally everyone except for you. Why do you think gay guys love this shit?"

Ash scoffed, "Where did Graves find a girl with a crucifix necklace? I'm Mexi-Catholic, and my abuela is the only person I know with a crucifix."

"We met at a party," Erinn said.

"You don't look like a party girl," Ash replied. "I'm going to call you God's Girl."

"Oh my God, rude." Angel side-eyed Ash.

"Why is that rude?" Erinn asked. "What is a God's Girl?"

"They're like Suicide Girls..." Angel hesitated, then clarified, since Erinn didn't know what they were either. "Alt girls, models with tattoos, emo hair like you, but a lot more naked."

Zack looked away from Guitar Hero for a second to question Angel. "Are you into alt girls now?"

"I like curves," Angel said, looking at Ash, "but I can't handle down there."

Ash tilted her head. "There's nothing wrong down there."

"It looks like a Xenomorph," Angel said as he wrapped his arm around the back of his head and hissed. "All dripping with acid n' shit. Like something's gonna pop out and get me."

As odd as the conversation was, Erinn enjoyed it. The crew was less intimidating than they'd been when they blocked the door and trapped her inside. Learning their names and seeing them joke together calmed her down.

"You look like you're feeling better," Zack said.

Erinn exhaled. "A little."

"Think you can handle some more?" Angel asked, offering her the pipe.

It felt like all the muscles in her body heard him ask and answered, yes. But *she* didn't want to. *What if it pushes me over the edge, and I die right here?* She was thinking it over when the lights went out, Guitar Hero died, and everything went quiet.

"What happened?" she asked.

"Fate didn't feed the M-power box again," Zack answered. "We're out of juice."

Without the music, the sound of flesh slapping sounded from Fate's room, followed by Lez's moans.

"So, what's going on with that whole situation?" Erinn asked. "Are Lez and Graves just roommates, because it felt like they were together..."

"Oh honey," Angel said. "No one is ever just roommates."

"So, why is Lez in there with Fate?"

The only reason Erinn went to the apartment was because she liked Graves. She liked him a lot. He wasn't the person she thought he was, but he deserved better than Lez cheating on him the second he left.

Zack offered Erinn the pipe again. "Why don't you take that hit?"

"I shouldn't."

Angel reached over and pet Erinn's head. "It's okay, honey, you know you want it."

She didn't want Angel to be right, but she wanted it bad. She had sympathy-frustration over what Lez was doing, and anger. But the idea of another hit brought instant relief to those feelings.

Meth was hard at first, but there was an undeniable power behind it. In a strange way, it made her feel confident and alive. Maybe she was looking at it wrong. The environment could've caused her bad reaction.

"I'll try a little more," she said.

Angel handed her a lighter. "That's where it's at, girl."

Using the lesson Graves gave her, she lit the bowl. As the crystal melted, the buzzing in her body intensified. It was as if the pipe put itself in her mouth. She braced herself for the hit and inhaled.

"That is good," she said as a plume of smoke escaped her lips.

Lez's muffled screams grew louder. "Oh God. I'm cumming. Fuuuuuck."

Erinn didn't pass the pipe. She took another hit and decided out loud, "I don't like that bitch."

A grin spread across Angel's face. "Cute and crazy. I see why Graves likes her."

"I'm gonna tell him about this," Erinn said.

"I'm sure he knows," Zack said. "It's just the way things are."

"Yeah, well, I care about his feelings."

Erinn took her phone out, no longer feeling like a timid religious shut-in. She was ready to fight a bitch. A rush of emotions surged through her, and she liked it. She'd spent too many years being the "good girl," but now she felt like a badass. No way was she letting that slut fuck around on the guy she liked.

# The Pawnshop

## Graves

I dabbed the blood from my nose, then got out of the Dethbox. My phone buzzed. Erinn was calling, but I didn't want to talk.

Or maybe I didn't want to talk to her. There was a payphone outside the pawnshop. I almost walked past it, but I stopped, and I felt a hum in my arm. It was the same feeling I got when I was craving meth, but this time I was craving revenge.

I popped the handset off the hookswitch and made an outbound call.

"911, what's your emergency?"

The sight of a child living with that psycho unsettled me. John's the one who needed to learn a lesson. *He* needed to lose something important. *He* was going to remember that night as much as I did.

"Are you able to speak?" the operator asked.

"Yeah."

"What's your emergency?"

"I'm calling to report an assault. There's a kid in the house, and the perp is a meth addict."

The operator's tone got serious. "Where did the incident occur?"

I stayed on the line long enough to provide John's address. Sure, the cops could track me down if they really wanted to but once they busted the guy, they wouldn't care about me.

I was feeling pretty good when I strolled up to the pawnshop, and this time, I answered my phone when it rang.

"Lez is cheating on you," Erinn blurted out.

My finger hovered over the pawnshop's intercom. "It's not what you think," I told her, holding the phone between my ear and shoulder. "Lez is probably just blowing Fate for drugs or some shit."

"What?!"

"BJ's are currency...I dunno, it's a whole thing, I just—"

"Whatever," Erinn said. "Those were not dick-sucking noises she was making."

And just like that, the glow I had from doing something good was stolen.

Maybe some people don't draw a line between sucking dicks and getting fucked, but we made a deal and she didn't stick to it. I'm not sure if I was jealous or just angry. Whatever it was, it felt awful and it wasn't helping my head. I slammed my fist into the pawnshop door.

The security camera above the door whirred, its lens trained on me.

"Not only that," Erinn added. "But everybody knows and nobody fucking cares."

"I invite one girl over..."

The camera whirred again, like it was zooming in on me. I was still bleeding from the nose where John decked me. Plus, I did punch their door. It was late, and the shop was getting ready to close for the night.

"Look, this guy's gonna call the cops on me. I need to go."

I waved at the camera and pressed the buzzer.

A voice crackled through the intercom. "What do you want?"

"Money," I said, holding up the crucifix.

The camera whirred again. A second later, a heavy click sounded and the barred door unlocked.

Old tools, camcorders, and TVs lined the aisles. Behind the counter, a ragged-looking pawnbroker grinned at me. He was a big guy, with skin like leather, and a wad of chew tucked in his cheek.

"Guessin' you need this money pretty bad," he said, licking his lips.

"I'm not desperate or anything."

The pawnbroker put a scale on the counter, then set a flat black slab next to it. "Let's see what it's worth," he said.

I gave him my necklace. "Eighteen karats, check the clasp."

The pawnbroker weighed the necklace. It came in at twelve grams. Then he scraped the pendant and chain on the black stone, leaving behind two golden streaks, and dripped some test acid on both.

"See that," he said, shaking his head.

The acid was fizzing hard. "Lots of bubbles," I said.

The broker turned his head and spat into a trashcan. "Closer to ten karats, probably plated."

"That's not right."

"Look kid." He let out a heavy sigh, like he was doing me a favor or something. "I'll give you fifty to pawn it, sixty-five to sell."

"That's bullshit. It's worth way more."

The pawnbroker packed his tools beneath the counter. "Let's be real for a second," he said. "How much do you need?"

"Two-hundred," I lied.

He smiled, putting his brown teeth on display. "You're not getting two hundred. What's the minimum you need," he asked again, pointing at my face. "To get yourself out of whatever mess you're in."

"A hundred."

The pawnbroker slapped a carbon copy sales receipt on the counter and handed me a pen. At least a hundred would keep me out of trouble with Fate.

I walked out with the cash, hopped in the Dethbox, and took stock of my situation. At that moment, I had a couple of shards, I'd dealt with an asshole, I was alive, and I wasn't any deeper in debt. There was just one thing I needed to verify with Fate.

Does John know where you live?

You think I'd give that psychopath my address?

Good. We need to cut contact.

It was time to deal with the next problem, Lez. There was no good way to approach that shitstorm, but meth would help. I put a stolen shard in my palm and crushed it. Then I snorted it up my good nostril and headed back to Fate's.

Erinn was spinning a bowl when I walked in. She must've bought more, which was a surprise given how she'd acted earlier, but that's meth for you.

The crew were on their toes, watching her burn through the hit like they were watching their souls leave their bodies, and she showed no signs of stopping. By the time she finished, the bowl was cashed.

"What happened to your face?" she asked, coughing on the smoke.

"Nothing, I—"

"Liar," Erinn said, then rapid-fired a follow-up. "Where's your necklace?"

"How did even you notice that?"

"'Cause she's obsessed with you," Lez, who looked ready to punch a bitch, snapped.

Erinn smirked. "At least I'm not cheating on him."

At that moment, the crew were distancing themselves from the conflict by pretending to have side conversations.

"Tonight sucked," I said to Lez. "If you couldn't tell from the bloody nose and black eye that no one but Erinn seems to care about."

"And?" Lez asked.

"I'm tired. Just be honest with me about Fate."

"Nothing is going on." Lez stole glances at the crew, making sure they wouldn't talk, I assumed. "You're gonna take her word over mine?"

"I don't think she'd lie to me."

Lez grabbed her supplies. "Take me home. I'm done with this bitch."

Take me home—that comment hit me.

Lez was my foundation. It didn't matter if she was cheating on me. There was nowhere else for me to go, and nothing else for me to do. At the end of the day, I lived with Lez and I worked for Fate. And when she asked me to take her home, it was my job to drive her there, regardless of how I felt.

"You're gonna ditch me for that slut?" Erinn asked as I followed Lez out.

"I'm her ride."

"I've been waiting to talk to you all night."

"I have to deal with this," I told her. "You drove yourself. No one is forcing you to stay."

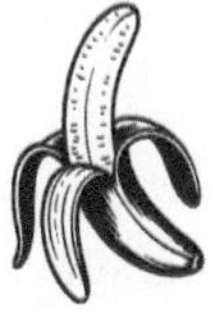

Lez sat in the passenger seat, quietly lighting a square of tinfoil. The tarry ball of heroin on it smoked as she inhaled its toxic vapors. I knew meth wasn't any better, but I hated heroin. It put Lez to sleep while I was awake and stole her memory when we needed to talk about shit.

"That's enough," I said, cracking the window.

Lez shot me a glance as the smoke whipped around her. "Close the fucking window, you're wasting it."

"I can't believe you've been sleeping with Fate."

"I'm not sleeping with Fate. Your girlfriend's just trying to start shit."

"She's not my girlfriend," I said.

"Sure seems like it."

"I skimmed meth off Three-Eyed John," I said to change the subject. "We can smoke tonight if you tell me what's going on. I'm the only person who can fuck you, remember that?"

Lez curled into a ball, huddling over her tinfoil square to stop the wind from stealing the smoke. With her head between her knees, she lit up again, breathing in the little vacuum she'd created for herself.

When we got home, she was so far gone I had to pull her out of the passenger seat and walk her to the apartment, but I never expected Backslash would be waiting for us when we got to the door.

"What happened to Jenna?" Backslash demanded.

Lez stumbled up to her. "Get the fuck away from my apartment."

"Maybe I'll point the cops in your direction," Backslash said. "Graves had her bracelet, which means you both know what happened."

I pulled Lez back and stepped up. "What cops?"

"Oh, I dunno." Backslash shoved me. "The cops who arrest people."

"Look, we didn't do anything," I said. Obviously, I couldn't tell her Jenna overdosed on my watch, or that I helped dump her body in the trash. "What are the cops asking you about?"

Backslash sucked in a breath and looked at me like she was about to hit me. "I filed a missing person's report after that bullshit story you gave me."

Lez turned to me, looking worried.

"What did they say?" I asked Backslash.

"Why did you have Jenna's bracelet?" she asked, tearing up. "What'd you do to her?"

"It's her own fault," Lez muttered.

Backslash reeled back and slapped Lez in the face. "Don't ever talk about her like that again. The cops found where you dumped her body because you shitheads buried her with her phone in her pocket."

My heart dropped into my stomach. "You don't understand."

"Lucky for you," Backslash said. "I didn't tell them her car is still parked behind Fate's apartment complex."

"Oh shit," Lez mumbled, deep in thought. "I like... totally forgot. She didn't park in front because she's paranoid."

"Are you both fucking braindead?" Backslash yelled.

I may not have thought about Jenna's stuff. But I knew why Backslash didn't rat us out. If Fate went down for Jenna, he would take us all down with him. The question was, did Jenna have anything on her phone that could incriminate us or was she careful enough to be vague?

"Do they suspect anything?" I asked.

"That's all you care about?" Backslash said; she was fighting back tears.

"I didn't do anything," I explained. "Jenna stole—"

Backslash decked me before I could finish explaining what happened. My face was still raw from John's assault. Adrenaline hit my nerves and before I knew it, I had Backslash up against the wall the same way John pinned me.

"We didn't do anything to her," I said under my breath, hoping the neighbors couldn't hear us. "And I'm getting real sick of people hitting me in the face." I pressed my forearm into her neck, watching her skin change color. "It's time for you to fuck off and lose our numbers."

When I backed off, Backslash crumpled to her knees, her eyes locking onto mine with raw intensity. She didn't say shit, and she didn't need to. The betrayal was etched on her face.

Lez walked past her and into the apartment.

"Have fun with Fate's fucktoy," Backslash muttered, pushing herself up.

I avoided her gaze as I went inside and locked the door behind me. That day couldn't have been any worse if it tried. And I hadn't even gotten to the point of discussing the thing that pissed me off the most.

"Backslash called you Fate's fucktoy," I said. "Wanna talk more about how you're not cheating on me?"

Lez maintained her guilty silence.

"I don't like feeling trapped," I said as I collapsed on the couch. "The cops are gonna figure out where Jenna was spending her time."

"They'll know she overdosed," Lez said. "It's fine."

"Fine? I don't have a place, or a job, and I'm indebted to a psychopath who's fucking my girlfriend behind my back."

"If it makes you feel better," Lez said, her lips curling into a smile. "He was fucking me behind my back."

"Are you capable of taking anything seriously?"

"That's your fucking problem." Lez came at me with renewed energy. "You take things way too seriously. Fate gets me high, and I like getting high. So, if I fuck him, then I don't have to pay money or make someone else pay."

"Why am I even here?"

"No one's forcing you to stay here," Lez said. "You act like I haven't done anything for you. Do you see me out at raves or parties anymore? No, because you're here with me every day, so just leave if you hate it so much."

"Sounds great, know anyone who wants a drug dealing roommate who can't afford to pay rent?"

Instead of answering, she got up, took her top off, and strutted towards the bedroom. Then she stopped in the doorway and shot her "fuck me" eyes over the shoulder. That's how she dealt with conflict.

And like a moth to the flame, I followed, unable to resist. I wanted to be pissed off, but that body... and those drugs. Neither allowed for the proper processing of emotion. Lez had hijacked my brain, and she knew it, because she was waiting for me on the bed with her legs spread and a finger in her pussy.

"Fate's load made my panties all messy."

I glared at her, hard as rock. "Why the fuck would you say that?"

"It turns you on."

"It's fucking disgusting," I shot back, but I couldn't turn away. Maybe I did like it. I didn't know what to think anymore. All I knew was I was horny. "Just keep your fucking mouth shut and let's do this."

I wrapped my hand around her neck and squeezed until she couldn't speak. Her eyes bulged. Then she smiled and licked her teeth as her face went flush and the veins in her neck swelled.

Fate must've fucked her good because I slid right in. As I pumped in and out, white foam developed around my dick, collecting and running down her pussy to her asshole. The lack of friction combined with the meth let me thrust as hard and fast as I wanted without blowing my load early.

"Is that all you got?" she choked.

I let go of her neck and slapped her. The pressure swelled inside me as I thrust harder and deeper.

"Come on," she moaned. "Fuck me like you mean it."

The pressure came to a head. My dick was so swollen I could feel the outline of each vein pressing into her pussy. I passed the point of no return, pulled out, then pushed my dick back inside as I came.

"See how much hotter that was," she said, catching her breath. "You worry too much about shit that doesn't matter."

I collapsed onto the bed, and at least for a moment, I felt better. Lez wasn't worried about Backslash, or the cops, or feelings. She did whatever she wanted, and she always had a good time. Maybe I could get past feelings too. Because all the rules I grew up with, all those conventions and social mores, they weren't real.

# Ditching the Evidence

Ash jammed a bent wire between the weatherstripping and driver's side window of Jenna's car. Her lips twisted as she maneuvered the wire, hoping to snag the door lock so we could get inside.

"Why are we doing this?" I asked her.

"We don't want this car anywhere near us," she said as the lock popped.

"I mean like, why us? Me and you. Why are *we* doing this?"

Ash opened the driver's door and tossed the wire inside. "I know how to jimmy a lock, and Lez wanted you to have my back."

She pressed the unlock button, and all the doors clicked. Then she motioned for me to get in the passenger side. The stale air of leather hit me when I leaned in. As I sat back in the seat, my stomach sank. There was a faint scent of perfume beneath the must, and it smelled just like Jenna had on the night we buried her.

"Zack didn't look happy about us going together," I said.

Ash pulled a flathead screwdriver from her pocket. There was a subtle click as she popped it into a slot next to the gearshift. She knew a thing or two about cars. There was an override button hidden beneath the plastic. She cast a look at me as she pressed the button, stepped on the brakes, and then shifted into neutral.

"Lez likes things a certain way," she said. "Now get out and push."

I got out of the car, checked for any spectators, and then closed the door. Ash and I locked eyes as I pushed on the grille. It looked like she was checking me out. Then she cut the wheel, navigating out of the tight spot.

Once we cleared the other cars, I sprinted to the rear, straining as I pushed it through another turn. And that was the easy part. Next, I had to get her across the main road and into a neighborhood without getting hit. Anywhere, even a street away, was better than keeping the car in Fate's complex.

We waited for the traffic to clear, but as soon as we pushed out, an unmarked Charger rounded the intersection, taking a right on red, and it spotted us. The distinct chirp of a siren sounded, and I held my breath as the white sedan blocked the road in front of us.

"Need a hand?" the officer asked as he stepped out.

What else could I say? "Yea," I called back and pointed. "Just need to get to the house across the street."

The officer shielded his eyes from the sun and scouted the neighborhood. "Hold on," he said as he walked into the middle of the street and waved his arms to stop the traffic flow.

Once we had a clear shot to the neighborhood, the officer ran to the back of Jenna's car and pushed with me. There I was, a drug-dealing tweaker, side by side with a cop. There was no word to describe it other than horrifying.

My heart was pounding, and each limb felt like it was about to give way. I thanked God when we cleared the traffic and Jenna pressed the brakes, steering us in front of a random house.

The officer ran back to his car, and I exhaled. But the relief was short-lived. He turned on the sirens and slowly crossed the road, pulling to a stop just behind us. I leaned against the license plate and said a prayer.

"What's the matter with it?" the officer asked as his boots hit the ground.

"Bad battery," I lied.

I could feel the intensity of Ash's glare burning through the rearview mirror. We didn't even have the keys. As soon as the cop realized that, we were screwed, and I'd just offered up a problem he wanted to solve.

"Pop the hood," he said, being obnoxiously helpful.

Ash must've heard his command through the window because the hood popped a second later. The officer grabbed jumper cables from his trunk and handed them to me with a reassuring smile.

"It's okay," I told him. "We'll be fine."

The officer didn't accept my plea. He reached into the gap above the grille, but before he could release the secondary latch, an urgent call crackled over his radio.

"Code 3, officer needs assistance at 19th Avenue and Camelback Road."

With that, the officer snatched his cables back, tossed them in his trunk, and sped off. Ash nodded to me in the rearview mirror and I pushed her deeper into the neighborhood.

"What did you mean before?" I asked as jumped back into the passenger seat. "When you said Lez likes things a certain way."

Ash's fingers glided across the console before landing on my thigh, inching their way up until her intentions were clear. "This is her way of making up for Fate," she said, rubbing her hand on my crotch until my dick was bulging through my blue jeans. "Kinda like a freebie."

"What about Zack?"

With a careless shrug, Ash's fingers worked at the button on my pants.

"I'm just surprised," I said, scooting away from her. "She was pissed at Erinn."

"Lez views Erinn as a threat to the order," Ash muttered, her breath hot on my neck as she unzipped my fly and climbed over the console. "Lez can't control Erinn. She doesn't want her putting ideas in your head."

"But she's fine with us hooking up?"

"You don't look at me the way you look at Erinn. It's different."

Ash climbed on top of me, and we did something I never thought I'd do—fucked in the back of a dead girl's car. Jenna's scent lingered in my nostrils. And like most situations I'd found myself in, I was both confused, uncomfortable, and horny.

If Ash was my consolation prize for having a slutty girlfriend, I didn't hate it. The rules were confusingly simple. Sell drugs, take drugs, buy drugs. Repeat. Fuck Lez, get cheated on, fuck Ash. Repeat. Everyone knew, but nobody talked about it.

There was only one rule: leave Erinn alone. Don't mess with the order.

# A Month Later

## Erinn

Erinn rubbed concealer under her bloodshot eyes. The dark blue bags lightened, blending in with her surrounding skin. Then, leaning into the vanity, she tore through her tangled hair. A clump detached from her scalp, clinging to her fingers.

"Oh my God," she shuddered. "Gross."

She wiped the oily strands into her wastebasket and stared at her reflection, watching her eyes cloud over.

The round, youthful skin that used to pad her smile now hung from her cheekbones, pulling her lips into a tired frown. She shrieked, punched the mirror, and watched the fracture spread like a dark vein through the glass.

Her knuckles dripped blood onto the carpet below, but she didn't feel anything.

All she could feel was a burning command coursing through her veins—MORE. Meth to stay awake, meth to focus, meth to keep her sane. But meth was the one thing she couldn't have anymore. Everything she thought she knew had just been turned upside down, and the only path ahead was abstinence.

"What the fuck was that?" Chels asked from the doorway.

Erinn hid her bloody hand behind her back. "I fell into the mirror."

Chels took a cautious step over the discarded wrappers and trash that littered Erinn's floor. "We need to talk," she said, scrunching her nose. "What the fuck is going on with you?"

"Nothing," she said. "I just hate my face."

"Okay," Chels spoke with an air of superiority. An indignant tone she'd developed over the past month. "Do you think that has anything to do with the fact that you're not sleeping anymore or spending all your time out with that Graves person, doing whatever it is you do?"

Erinn balled her hand into a fist. "I knew you were going to find a way to make it about him."

"The guy's a fucking loser." Chels crossed her arms. "And I care about you. But if you think you can trash my house, then turn around and disrespect me, you can fuck right the hell off."

"You mean our house?"

"Hmmm, I feel like you have to pay for it if you want to call it ours."

"I haven't gotten paid yet."

"Do you still have a job?" Chels' neck stiffened as she waited for a response.

Erinn hadn't been to work, not since she started smoking meth. There was no room in her schedule for a job. Every muscle ached with desire, a deep and demanding thrum that made her want to scream. She couldn't imagine life without meth, but she had to face it.

She knew Graves didn't want her at Fate's. She didn't bother waiting for his invitation. She went back to the apartment on her own, against his wishes, and she couldn't stop going.

"Graves doesn't even want me over there," Erinn said, feeling a flood of emotion well up inside her chest and spill over into tears as her chest heaved. "I dunno what I'm doing, Chels."

Chels relaxed her stance. She was probably relieved to hear that things between Erinn and Graves were failing.

"Look," she said. "I don't even know the guy. But I know you, and you were a different person before you met him."

"I'm still the same person," Erinn sobbed.

"This is not how normal people live," Chels said, scooping a Taco Bell wrapper off the floor. She held it at a distance as hard cheese and brown lettuce fell out.

"I'll clean."

"You better," Chels said. Her tone was sharp as she tossed the crumpled wrapper into Erinn's wastebasket.

Erinn's gaze shot to the basket, her eyes quickly returning to Chels'.

Chels paused, then looked back at the basket. "You almost jumped out of your skin."

"I don't like you touching my stuff."

Chels knelt and reached her hand into the basket, wrinkling her nose at the smell. There was a Clearblue pregnancy test, nestled in a clump of hair. She wiped the hair off of it and squinted at the result window.

"You know I peed on that, right?" Erinn asked.

"There's a blue line on it." Chels' face was caught between pity and excitement. "Is this why you've been so weird lately?" she asked, breathing a sigh of relief. "I thought you were on drugs or something. How long have you known, and why haven't you talked to me?"

Thankful for the excuse, Erinn seized the opportunity to blame her behavior on being pregnant, even though she'd only found out herself.

"I don't know what the fuck to do, Chels. I'm freaking out, and I lost my job, and I don't know what the fuck I'm gonna do."

"Is it Graves'? Did you talk to him?"

Erinn shook her head. "It's his, but I don't know how to tell him. He's dating someone else," she said, letting out an exasperated laugh. "And she's the worst human being ever, and she's fucking cheating on him, and then there's this girl Ash he's fucking and I'm just sitting there alone."

Chels looked mortified. “Whose place are you hanging out at?”

“This guy Fate.”

“Wow, okay. I have no idea what’s going on.” Chels tried to wrap her head around the situation. “So you’re hanging out with Graves and his girlfriend and some other girl he’s with at this Fate guy’s place. And then what? Then you can start a family together or something?”

“It sounds pretty stupid when you say it like that,” Erinn muttered.

“It’s fucking retarded.”

Erinn’s chest rose and fell as she panted. “I don’t know what the fuck to do.”

Chels put her hands on Erinn’s shoulders. “You need to get rid of this guy. Right now.”

# The Banana

## Graves

I missed the scent of sweet rot that used to linger in Fate's apartment. Meth fumes hung in the air, and tweakers sprawled out on the carpet below. The apartment made an unspoken promise in the beginning: that there would always be an abundance of drugs, but scarcity was the only constant.

Erinn ran to greet me as I walked in the door, with a ripe yellow banana clutched firmly in her hand. "Got you something."

"A banana?" I asked.

Without batting an eye, she handed me the fruit. "Do you like it?"

"I guess..."

"I got it just for you," she said.

"Why would you get me a banana?"

"I dunno, it's healthy," she said as she hurried beside me to the circle. "It was super cheap, too. We should have some more healthy things, ya know. I think it would be good for us."

"Us?"

Erinn nodded and grabbed my hand. "We should talk."

"Not now." I threw the banana on the floor and sat down next to it. "Do you know who has the pipe?" I asked, trying to control the spasms in my hand. "I'm coming down hard right now."

"I saved you a hit," Lez said.

I reached for the pipe, but before I could take it, my phone vibrated.

"For fuck's sake, what now?" I asked.

"After your call, we really need to talk," Erinn insisted.

All I could focus on was the tiny bit of crystal left in the pipe. Not Erinn's stupid-ass banana, or whatever else she wanted to talk about, or whoever was on the other end of that damn phone call.

"What do you want?" I said, putting the speaker to my ear.

A rude voice asked me to verify my name and address. If I had learned one thing from debt collection, it's that you never confirm your identity. That restarts the statute of limitations. And while I didn't have any debt that I knew of, there are plenty of other reasons I didn't want to give that bitch my info.

"He's not here," I told her. "Can I take a message?"

Lez and Erinn started arguing with each other while the woman on the phone droned on about needing to reach Ezekiel on a very important matter. As if anything mattered.

"Who are you even?" I asked the caller.

"This is Wanda with the Department of Economic Security."

"Take me off your list."

"There is no list," Wanda said flatly. She must've left her professional attitude at home that day. "This is the Department of Economic Security," she repeated. "And I need to reach Ezekiel Graves."

"What do you want?"

"We received a request for food stamps and—"

"I didn't make a request."

"As I was saying. We received a request for food stamps from a woman who identified Ezekiel Graves as the father of her minor child. The state is petitioning to establish paternity."

She had to be kidding... Eva, the chick who drove a Lexus and lived rent-free in a house gifted to her, was applying for food stamps?

"That's not even my kid."

Erinn's head snapped around. "You have a kid?"

"It's not his," Lez answered.

"Would you two shut the fuck up, please?" I said, glaring at them.

"Excuse me," Wanda shot back. "What did you just say?"

"Not you." I put the phone back to my ear. "Look, lady, I don't have a fucking kid. That walking disease masquerading as a woman is using the system. If you want to do your job, then deny her request."

"If the child isn't yours, then you should have no issue taking a paternity test."

"Fine, whatever."

"What is your current address?" Wanda asked.

"I'm not giving you that."

"We need to update our records and schedule you for paternity testing at an approved location. Once we confirm the test results, you'll receive a copy of the test at your address."

"6900 E. Azure Vista Way, Penthouse 902, Scottsdale, AZ 85255."

"Why are you giving my address?" Lez asked.

She tried to take the phone away from me. I put my elbow up to block her, but she jumped on top of me. I stayed on the line long enough to get the testing location before she stole the phone and hung up.

"Calm your fucking tits," I told her. "It was the Department of Economic Security. They want to come after me for child support, and I just need to get a mouth swab so I can put this shit behind me."

Erinn was vibrating, like she couldn't contain herself. "It sounds like you have a kid."

"Pipe," I said to Lez.

Lez handed me the pipe while explaining the situation to Erinn. "My ex-boyfriend Ryder, cucked Graves with his ex-girlfriend, Eva. Like I said, he doesn't have a kid."

I spun the bowl and sucked the smoke deep into my lungs. I'd almost forgotten about Sadie altogether, and now she was back again, haunting me. Memories raced through my mind while sweat trickled down my forehead. I exhaled, anticipating a wave of euphoria, but all I felt was tension.

"You're taking the test," Erinn said to me. "You might be a parent."

"It was stupid to think I ever could've been one."

"You're about to find out for sure, though." Erinn moved in for a hug, her arms open, as Lez gritted her teeth.

"I'm not gonna take the test," I told her. "I can't."

"Then why the fuck did you give them my address?" Lez asked, wedging herself between me and Erinn.

I shrugged and passed Erinn the pipe, but she didn't take a hit.

She passed the pipe to Ash. The strangeness of that particular action was enough to shift my focus away from Sadie. No one passed on meth, not when the bowl was nearing the end.

"Are you okay?" I asked Erinn.

"I'm just focused on you right now," she said. "You shouldn't drive when you're this stressed, but you need to take the test before you talk yourself out of it. I'll take you there myself."

Lez stood, keeping herself between us. "You're not taking him anywhere."

"You're not gonna take him," Erinn stood and matched Lez's glare. "And he won't take himself. This is important. He needs to know whether he has a kid out there who needs him."

"Why the fuck do you care?" Lez asked.

Erinn opened her mouth to speak but stopped herself.

I was at a loss, unsure of my next move. "I'm gonna go with Erinn."

Lez's neck cracked as she whipped her head in my direction. "Let's talk," she hissed as she stormed out the door, pulling me by the collar. She slammed the door shut and shoved me against the wall. "I don't know what your deal is today, and I don't like where it's headed."

"Where what's headed?"

"I'm going to be very clear right now. You're not allowed to fuck Erinn."

"Right, you can just fuck Fate whenever."

"I fuck Fate because he gets me high. You know what it's like to come down. You know you'd do anything to stay spun. That girl isn't giving you anything. This is not the same thing."

"At least she's nice to me."

"I swear to God," Lez said. "I don't like that bitch. I don't like that you brought her here, and I don't like that she never left. If you so much as think about fucking her, you will fucking regret it."

I rode with Erinn just to piss Lez off, and I already regretted it. Not because I didn't like Erinn, but because I didn't want to take that damn test. I already knew the answer. My entire life was already molded to the answer.

"Don't speed," I muttered, without looking at Erinn.

There was a white Dodge Charger tailing us. It looked just like the unmarked cruiser from last month. Its slanted mirrors stared at me in the side-view mirror, like two menacing eyes.

Erinn's body tensed, and the sudden jerk of her muscles caused the car to swerve.

"Is it a cop?" she asked.

"I don't know yet."

"It's probably nothing," she said. "Like the license plate thing where you keep seeing triple sixes... meth messes with your head."

We both waited, staring at the mirrors, but no lights flashed, and no sirens sounded. I wasn't sure if it was a cop, but I was suspicious of every Charger. Especially white Chargers following too close.

I kept my eyes on the mirror for the duration of the drive, but when we pulled into the testing facility, the Charger kept driving straight.

"Did you catch the plate?" Erinn asked.

I shook my head.

"Me neither." She shifted into park. "Well, we're here now."

The testing facility was a small brick building, but it loomed over me. With every step, my heart pounded. By the time we reached the door, it felt like a jackhammer. I stopped and knelt, worried I might faint.

Then I felt Erinn's hand touching my back, and my pulse slowed. Her fingers traced my vertebrae, sending shivers down my spine, igniting a sensation of security I hadn't felt in ages.

I took her hand and opened the glass door. We walked through it together, and I signed in while she picked a spot to sit.

The office was crowded, and chatty. Other people made my skin crawl. I didn't realize how hard it was to exist outside of the circle. I no longer felt welcome, safe, or comfortable out in the real world.

"What are you thinking about?" Erinn whispered as I sat beside her.

I didn't answer her directly, but the questions in my mind were 'who am I, and how did I get here?'

The drugs freed me from pain, fear, and regret. Until they didn't. I was free until some outside force made me think about the things I was ignoring. Like Wanda and the stupid-ass Department of Economic Security.

What if, by some chance, Sadie was mine?

"My ex took Sadie away from me," I said, confiding in Erinn. "She lied about me being abusive, and I lost everything."

"When was that?"

"Before this all started," I told her.

"Is that why you're doing drugs and hanging out at Fate's?"

"I don't want to take this test."

"We're already here," Erinn said. "There's no backing out now."

"I could send someone in my place. Then there's no chance of a positive match. Sadie would keep living her life and never have to see me. She'd never need to know who I am now."

Erinn brushed a strand of hair from her face, her eyes locked on mine.

"I bet you were a great dad," she said.

"Ezekiel Graves," the technician called my name.

"Ezekiel?" Erinn laughed—she had no idea what my name was.

I stood and faced the technician, realizing that even the people closest to me didn't know anything about me.

"It's Zeke," I said, addressing Erinn and the technician. "And I can't be here."

Erinn stood and slipped her fingers between mine, igniting that forgotten protection and warmth inside of me again. She stayed by my side as we followed the technician through the hall and into the testing room, with its solitary chair. I waited in the lone chair while the technician prepped a swab. Then, I shut my eyes, opened my mouth, and prayed for the best.

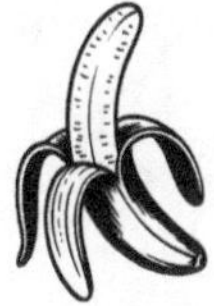

"Any sign of that car?" Erinn asked.

After checking the side-mirror, I turned around to get a better view of what was behind us. There was no sign of the Charger. Objectively, I knew meth caused paranoia, and the crew always tried to stop themselves from spiraling into theories. But it wasn't crazy to think that someone could be following us. We were addicts, drug runners, and Backslash could've pointed a finger in Fate's direction when the cops asked her about Jenna.

"Still can't believe what happened to Jenna," I mumbled.

Erinn came to a stop at the light. "I thought your daughter's name was Sadie."

"First of all, Sadie isn't my daughter, and secondly, Jenna is..." I realized Erinn hadn't been there for Jenna's overdose, and no one talked about her either. "Jenna's just someone I used to know."

"Like an ex?"

"I barely even knew the girl."

The light turned green, and Erinn took off. "I think there's too much on your mind," she said. "You pretend things don't bother you, like your daughter, or this Jenna girl, but that doesn't stop them from bothering you. And I see the look on your face sometimes. You look broken."

I put my feet up on the passenger seat and rested my head between my knees. "I just need to get spun." But then I looked at Erinn—her eyes were tired like mine, but unlike mine, they were searching for something better.

Erinn parked in front of Fate's, but she didn't open her door.

"Maybe you should find a better way to cope," she said. "I know you don't believe that you have a daughter, but there's a chance you do."

"Is that why you didn't smoke?" I asked. "Finding a new way to cope."

"Trying to."

"Then what are you still doing at Fate's?"

I could tell that question hit hard.

"You know I like you," she said. "We don't have to live like this anymore, and you don't have to be with Lez."

It's not like I hadn't thought about being a normal person, and what being with Erinn, who actually gave a shit about me, would be like. Maybe, just maybe, we could be something more than this.

"I'm trapped though, and not just metaphorically."

"So what, then?" Erinn's pitch changed. Her voice grew urgent. "You're just going to go back in there and keep digging your grave? We don't have to end up like those fucking losers."

"You're kinda being a bitch," I said, swinging the door open.

Erinn got out and slammed her door shut. "I didn't choose this. You brought me here."

I kicked the passenger door shut. "Then go. No one wanted you here anyway. You just kept showing up."

Erinn froze, paralyzed by the comment.

I think a part of me wanted her to leave while she still could, she just needed a push to get her going. It was no secret that she hung around for me, and it'd be better for everyone if she just walked away.

"Please tell me someone has crystal," I said as I walked into Fate's apartment.

Ash looked up from the circle. There was a syringe in her hand, and a water bottle, a tourniquet, gauze, and mini band-aids by her side.

"What did I just walk in on?" I asked.

"Are you gonna judge me too?" she asked. "Suppliers are dry right now, and we're all broke. We need to make every bit count."

"Six months," Zack told her. "That's life expectancy once you start slamming."

The door opened and shut. Erinn walked up behind me. She tugged at my arm, visibly shaken by the needle.

Ash maintained her focus against the opposition. "Stop being such bitches. I bought this batch. And if anyone wants to share it, this is how."

She ground her bag of crystals into a fine powder. Then she transferred the meth into an empty container, added some water from the bottle, and swirled it around until the crystal had dissolved.

Lez excused herself from the circle and headed to Fate's room.

Erinn twisted my arm and whispered in my ear. "Let's get out of here."

I broke free from her grasp, but before I could consider the options, Fate marched out of his room and smacked the back of Ash's head.

"Pack up your shit and get out," he demanded.

Ash ignored him.

"Are you deaf?" Fate snatched the syringe from her hand and threw it into her purse with the supplies. "We're not hiding another body. If you wanna die, do it somewhere else."

"Another body?" Erinn asked.

Ash stumbled past us as Fate shoved her towards the door. "I don't have anywhere to go," she yelled.

"Graves will take you somewhere."

Erinn stood in front of me. "I don't want you around her and her needles."

"Don't worry about him." Lez walked by and grabbed my hand, pulling me towards the door where Ash was waiting. "He won't be alone. He'll be with me. We'll drop Ash somewhere she can shoot up."

"Come on, Zack," Ash demanded. "We're leaving."

Zack didn't move though. He glared at me, then Ash, and stayed put.

I turned back to Erinn. "You never belonged here. I think it's a good time to walk away."

The Dethbox let out an unsettling growl as it chugged along, followed by knocking. I pounded the dash, as if that would help, and breathed a sigh of relief when the frame stopped vibrating and let me think again.

The last thing I needed right now was for the car to break down and leave us stranded. With our luck, some well-intentioned cop would come along to help, and we'd all wind up in prison.

"Turn up there," Lez said.

Ash rolled her eyes. "Where are you even taking me?"

Lez unbuckled so she could turn around and face Ash in the back seat. "There's this guy Billy. He won't care if you slam at his place."

I tried to ignore the triple six on the license plate ahead of us as I turned the corner and headed into the neighborhood, but we were surrounded by run-down houses with busted-out windows.

Erinn had been blowing up my phone since we left. I imagine she was texting me not to shoot up, and to drive safe, and to think of the kid that wasn't even mine.

Lez tapped my shoulder. "This is Billy's place."

I pulled over, hoping to avoid temptation by staying in the car. But Lez glanced at me expectantly, like she wanted me to get out too. I didn't want to drop Ash off there, let alone go inside, but I got out anyway.

There was a camcorder watching us as we made our way through the overgrown yard. It was bolted into the stucco above the doorframe.

I pointed out the camera. "How tweaker is that?"

"Better than having to look through the blinds to see who's there," Lez said. "Have you seen tech shit lately? People are gonna start putting little fucking cameras in their doorbells soon."

Ash shuddered. "That's fucking crazy."

Lez grabbed the door handle and twisted. "It's open," she said, letting herself inside.

"Then what's the point of the camera?" I asked Ash.

She shrugged and followed us in. The first thing I noticed was the smell. It didn't smell like the sweet rot of Fate's. This was something else altogether, it reminded me of the dump on State Route 85.

Jenna's body flashed through my mind, right as my phone buzzed again. I needed to catch up on Erinn's texts.

> The crew just told me about Jenna, what the fuck?!

> Look, we really need to talk.

> Please don't do anything stupid.

I closed out of Erinn's messages and found a new one from Backslash.

> Fate always uses a burner, but the cops asked me point-blank if I knew who Jenna would've been texting with.

Lez stole my attention. "Are you coming?"

I pocketed the phone, lifted my shirt to my nose, and walked deeper into Billy's place. The words *fuck*, *bitch*, and *trash* were scrawled on the wall. Nearby sections of drywall had been torn down, exposing the decayed wooden beams and mineralized pipes beneath.

A roach scurried out from the wooden beams, its antennae twitching as it dodged the debris scattered across the floor.

Lez's foot came down on the roach with a sickening crunch. "Wake up, Billy."

Billy, who was out cold next to the roach guts, stretched, and licked his dry lips as he sat up. For someone with a camera bolted to his door, he was surprisingly unfazed by the intrusion. He first observed Lez, then turned to Ash and then to me, before being hospitable.

"Speedball for the ladies?" he asked.

"My dumbass friend needs a place to crash," Lez said.

Billy's lips cracked and bled when he smiled. "The girl I hope."

Ash went for it, plopping down on the floor next to Billy. "I'm not allowed to shoot up at their place," she said, placing her hand on his lap. "If you're cool with me slamming here, we can work something out."

That's all it took for Ash to assimilate—a place where she could shoot up. And she'd work out a sexual arrangement without her boyfriend's knowledge. Of course, it's not far from what her and I were already doing, and I think it hit me at that moment. None of this was far from what we were doing.

"We should go," I said to Lez.

She looked at me and laughed. "We're not leaving sober."

"But we don't slam, right? That's the whole reason we're dropping Ash off."

Lez whispered in my ear. "Fate's place can't turn into this place."

"Because it's bad," I said.

"We can handle ourselves," Lez said. "Don't worry so much about stupid shit."

I wanted to tell her she was crazy, but I was wracked with come down pangs, and Erinn kept buzzing my phone, adding to my stress. Not to mention Fate was under the microscope, and meth was scarce.

Lez joined Ash and tapped her arm again. "You owe us for finding you a place."

"Fine, bitch." Ash unzipped her kit and tied Lez off.

Lez clenched her fist. Her veins bulged into twisted ropes across her arm. Perfect little blue lines waiting for penetration.

Ash pricked the head of the needle into Lez's arm. A brownish piece of dried blood on the needle's shaft caught Lez's skin, blocking the needle's progression until the crust pushed through, entering her bloodstream.

Lez's eyelids fluttered.

"This is fucking heaven," she said.

Ash pulled the tourniquet off Lez's arm. "You're up, Graves."

"Do you have any clean needles?" I asked.

"I've used all of them," Ash admitted. "You realize you're fucking both of us, right?"

"I still don't want to die from an infected wound."

"Stop being a little bitch," Lez said. "I'm not leaving until you do it."

She laid back in the filth and spread her arms, making a trash angel on the floor. Bugs scattered from the mold-covered garbage. I couldn't stomach another second of that place, and I couldn't let Lez stay there either.

I took the needle and used my thumbnail to dislodge the dried blood, then I used my shirt to wipe the fresh blood away. Ash took the needle back to draw up the concoction while Lez tied me off.

Heart pounding, I watched veins rise to the surface of my arm. Panic and anticipation tangled inside me, sharp as the needle's bite.

A blast of icy liquid pierced my skin, chilling my veins. My body seized as if it had been flash-frozen. I coughed. There was a tingle in my spine, followed by a rush of heat that turned my face red and caused my muscles to spasm.

"Oh, fuck!"

"You good there?" Ash asked.

"Good?" I asked, realizing my panicked thoughts were gone. "Who even needs sex? If an orgasm had sex with a cumshot, and had a meth baby, this is how that baby would taste."

"Well, that didn't make any sense," Ash said. "My turn."

While Lez tied Ash off, I got lost in the experience. The perpetual fatigue that clung to me from all the sleepless nights was washed away. The pain of a hundred scrapes, cuts, and bruises vanished without a trace. The worries about Sadie, the horrors of watching Jenna die, gone.

Then my phone buzzed again, it was Erinn.

Is everything okay?

You need to chill the fuck out. I can handle myself.

Lez smirked, peeking over my shoulder. "Erinn won't even want to fuck with you once she finds out about this."

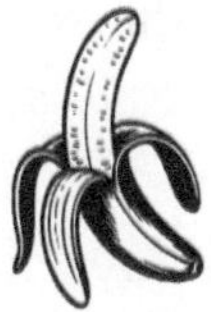

The Dethbox's engine roared as I tore over the tarmac. Every action felt electric and intensely alive. In that heightened state, I swear I could feel each pebble on the road.

"Slow the fuck down." Lez clutched the "oh shit" handle above the passenger window. She turned to look behind us, then sat down and pressed her back flat against the seat. "Slow down right now."

My eyes shot to the rearview mirror. The slanted headlights of a white Dodge Charger stared back at me. I felt a lump rise in my throat. The car moved in on us until the headlights disappeared from view. The windshield was tinted black, and I couldn't get a look at who was driving.

"Do you have anything on you?" I asked.

"I always have a piece," Lez said. "And there's residue in it."

"Why aren't they pulling us over?" I said, looking back. "Maybe it's not a cop."

The white sedan slowed down, its grille filling the rearview again. The headlights were vile-looking, almost alive, and glaring like they knew what we'd done. And who we were. If the car knew we were criminals, the driver had to know. I wiped my forehead and waited for the siren, but it never came.

Lez peered out the back. "It's just an asshole."

"Stop looking!"

There was an ominous clunk from under the Dethbox's hood.

My hand jerked, causing the car to veer. The meth had already caused a cascade of chemical reactions in my body. Adding a new flood of adrenaline and cortisol to the mix was proving unmanageable. Both my hands were white, clutching the wheel for dear life while my arms shook and sweat poured down my face.

"I need to pull over."

Lez looked back again. "Are you fucking kidding me?"

"Maybe he won't follow."

There was a Circle K gas station up ahead. Using all my strength and focus, I activated the turn signal and moved into the center lane. The Charger followed behind, closing in. We were bumper to bumper as I waited for the traffic to pass.

My chest rose and fell in erratic bursts. Tears joined the sweat on my face as my body attempted to flush the cortisol from my system. Lez was drumming a beat on her leg, glaring at the side-mirror.

"That car followed me and Erinn the other day."

Lez stopped drumming and stared at me. "And you didn't say anything?"

The traffic cleared, allowing me to turn into the Circle K. I pulled to an open pump. The Charger crawled around us and took a parking spot in front of the station. There it was, clear as day on the license plate. "G-"

Any license plate that starts with a G is a government-issued vehicle.

"Why's he just sitting there?"

"I dunno," Lez said. "Maybe we're just being paranoid. Were you even going that fast, or did it just feel like that?"

"I have no idea."

"Get out and pump some gas or something," she said.

The gas pump had a yellow bag over it and a sign that said out of order. If I acted like I parked there for gas, the cop would know I was tweaking. I couldn't just stand there either, so I walked into the station to grab a drink like a normal person. I'm sure Lez was losing her actual shit behind me, but I didn't look back.

As I surveyed the drink selection, the bell above the entrance rang. The cooler door offered a distorted reflection of the officer.

I grabbed a water bottle and walked to the counter. Then, I threw some money at the cashier and ran out.

Lez leaned her head out the window and slapped the door. "Let's go."

I turned the key, but the Dethbox sputtered. The dashboard lights flickered out. "Not now," I begged her. I pumped the gas and tried again. The engine sputtered and popped, then shut off. Gasoline fumes filled the air, my heart dropped into my gut, and the cop walked out.

"Smells like trouble." The officer said, walking up to us.

He rested his arm on the passenger sill and looked past Lez at me.

"Didn't I help you with a car before?" he asked.

I swallowed the lump in my throat and responded. "Old cars, ya know?"

The officer nodded, but his eyes weren't looking at me; they were scanning every inch of the Dethbox.

"Well," he said, pulling out his wallet. "Someone dropped this twenty on the counter inside..."

His statement caught me off guard. I didn't get any change from the clerk, but I can't remember the last time I'd had twenty bucks. It wasn't mine, was it? Was this guy messing with me? Had I even sped, or jerked the wheel?

I looked at Lez, wondering what was real and what was in my head.

"Are you just like, a nice cop?" I asked nervously.

He cocked his head, letting his mouth hang for a minute before asking if I was okay.

"I don't think that's my money," I told him.

The officer pursed his lips. "Okay then. I'm going to check the security cameras, and if this is yours, I'll give you a call. Give me your number and let me see your driver's license."

"That's not necessary, sir."

"I insist," he said.

He took my license and studied it, then pulled out a pen. "Ezekiel, my name is Officer Hallman. I'm ready to take down your phone number now, and I promise you I'll be in touch."

Once I gave him my number, he left.

Lez and I exhaled, for the first time since he walked up to us. The Charger drove away, and we stared at each other in silence until a text from Backslash came through.

Are you just ignoring me now?

"Do you think the cops are tailing us because of Backlash?" I asked Lez.

"No shit," she said.

"All these texts about Jenna...Backslash is probably trying to get a confession."

Lez clenched her fists and rocked back and forth on her seat. "I dunno what the fuck we're gonna do. But you cannot text that bitch. You can't use your phone either. And we can't drive this fucking car again. We need to get back to Fate's so we can figure this shit out now."

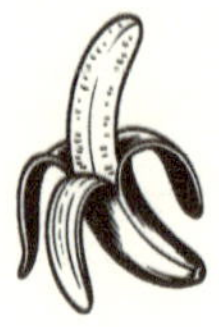

Fate threw my phone. The hard plastic ripped through his drywall and wedged firmly in place. Then he pulled the phone out of the wall, put it in the microwave, and hit start.

I opened the microwave and saved my phone before it exploded, and somehow it was still functional.

"I need my phone."

"Not here," Fate said. "Turn it off, or it's getting nuked."

I powered down the phone and shoved it in my pocket. It was hard to blame him. None of us knew how long I had been followed or how badly our operation had been compromised.

"How are we gonna make deliveries?" Fate asked, pacing.

"God's Girl has a car," Lez said with a glint in her eye.

Fate stopped in his tracks and gave Erinn a predatory glare.

"If Graves can come with me, it's a deal," Erinn said, a smirk playing on her lips as she stared at Lez.

"Deal," Fate said.

Lez narrowed her eyes at Erinn, but she bit her tongue. Someone had to be the driver. The choice was simple: risk the entire operation's failure or allow Erinn to take control with her conditions.

"Great," Lez said, clenching her jaw. "Thanks so much."

"Are you sure this is a good idea?" I asked Erinn. "You wanted to bail."

"Let's spin a bowl to celebrate," Lez interjected, slipping a dime bag out of her pocket. "I was saving a little something."

"Holding out is more like it," I said. "Let's fucking smoke."

Erinn put her hands out. "No thanks," she said. "I'm not feeling it right now."

"That's not a thing," Lez replied. "Considering we just got pulled over, acting like a narc is sketch as fuck. I saw you turn down that hit. If we're gonna trust you to drive for us, we need to know you're in."

"You don't have to smoke," I told Erinn.

Lez loaded the pipe and gave it to Erinn. "Yes, she does."

Erinn took the pipe. Her fingers trembled as she held it, and she barely spun it or inhaled any smoke.

"Graves." Lez pointed at the door. "I need to talk to you."

As soon as the door shut behind us, Lez's fake smile faded, and her voice got sharp.

"We need that bitch's car," she said. "Don't tell her that you slammed. She needs to keep liking you."

"Wasn't gonna."

"I don't want her messing with your head." Lez grabbed my crotch, tightening her grip until I could feel the beat of my heart through my balls. "She's not with us. She's only here for you."

"I know that."

Lez clenched her fist, sending pain through my stomach. "I don't like Fate... but you, you're in love with Erinn, and I need you to stay focused."

I choked down the pain-induced nausea. "Love is a strong word."

"I'm not retarded, dickhead. You don't look at me like you look at Erinn. You're always protecting her, no matter what." Lez mocked my voice. "Oh, I don't want to hurt poor Erinn. Oh, she shouldn't be involved in this kind of thing... Like everyone else here is a fucking loser but her."

## Lez's Gift

### Erinn

Erinn stared at her reflection. The meth had worn off, but the shame and the disappointment lingered. At one point, smoking felt like a choice, like a decision she could go back on, but not anymore.

Lez had gifted her a dime bag as a show of good faith, and it made the drive home with her.

"I'm pregnant," she said, clutching the baggie.

The initial thrill of smoking was gone, her baseline had shifted, and now smoking only brought her closer to remembering a sense of normalcy. It took the pain away, even though it was the root of her suffering.

"He doesn't even like me," she whispered as a tear rolled down her face. "I don't even like meth."

Chels knocked on her bedroom door.

"Go away," Erinn said.

"Are you gonna tell me what's wrong?" Chels asked.

Erinn didn't know if she had been talking out loud or in her head, whether her sobbing was quiet or loud, or if Chels was really standing on the other side of her door. Nothing felt real. The world was muted, her life unfolding like a movie she couldn't bring herself to watch.

As the lock twisted with a click, one of her questions was answered. Chels was real, and she was coming in. Erinn folded her fingers around the bag, hiding the truth from Chels.

Chels' eyes went straight to her hand. "What do you have?"

"Nothing."

"Are you still upset about what happened with Graves?" Chels took a step closer and placed her hand on Erinn's.

*She has no idea what I'm holding*, Erinn realized. *She thinks it's a keepsake or some shit I got from Graves.*

"He's the father of my kid," Erinn said. "I have to help him get better so he can be here for us."

"You don't have to do shit for him," Chels said. "Whatever's going on, I'm here for you."

"I don't think you are."

Chels folded her arms and narrowed her gaze. "Try me."

Erinn looked at her clenched fist and slowly turned her palm upwards, extending her fingers—she regretted it instantly.

"Wow," Chels said, taking a step back.

Tweakers are universally despised. Even tweakers don't like tweakers. And there Erinn was, holding a bag of meth. The drug from the billboards, the epidemic sweeping the state, right there in her hand.

Chels was wearing the same disgusted expression that had cut across her face when Graves offered them ecstasy at the party. That smug, self-righteous glare like she was better than everyone.

"Stop looking at me like that."

Chels glared harder. "You're fucking pregnant."

"You don't think I know that?"

"Obviously, you don't know what the fuck you're doing."

Erinn buried her face in her hands. "I was trying to throw it away before you barged in here to interrogate me."

"Try harder."

Chels left the bedroom and came back holding trash bags. "You've been nothing but shitty and distant lately," she said as she collected the garbage off the floor. "I tried to support you and help you, but this is crazy. You're not paying your bills cause you're smoking crack."

"It's meth."

"Well, excuse the fuck out of me." Chels handed Erinn an empty trash bag. "This one is for your clothes and anything else you want. Call your parents, or call a women's shelter, but leave me out of it."

"Can't we just talk?" Erinn asked.

"I've been doing nothing but trying to talk to you, and you don't care. I'm not gonna be a part of you killing your baby."

Erinn collected her band shirts and whatever was on top of her vanity. Makeup and empty gel bottles mostly. She didn't have much else. Nothing she could easily transport.

"My parents don't know I'm pregnant or that I'm strung out. Please," she begged Chels to give her one more chance. "I can't talk to them, and I don't have anyone else besides you."

"Well, I hope Graves was worth it."

Erinn slung the trash bag over her shoulder and stumbled out of the house. The door slammed behind her, and the lock clicked into place.

She collapsed into her car, flicked on the lights, and drove. Twenty minutes later, she cruised past a school, stopped in the middle of the street, and reversed into the parking lot.

There was a large, dim park with a baseball field, water fountains, and a playground. She walked along the edge of the field to avoid being seen by the kids hanging out after hours and headed down a gulley. Concealed by shadows was a culvert, a long concrete drainage tube, and the bars blocking it had been cut.

Any feelings of disgust she would've had for such a place were replaced by a desire to turn off the pain. She stepped into the culvert, letting the shadows consume her. The bugs scurrying around her feet lost their form to darkness. Feeling by touch, she walked deeper inside.

"Just a little," she told herself, pulling a shard from the bag.

# Forbidden Fruit

## Erinn - A few weeks later

Erinn pulled next to a Chrysler 300 and shifted her Smart car into park. Surprisingly little had changed since getting kicked out of Chels' place. Most of her time was spent at Fate's, driving drugs with Graves.

Her car was her home and her business. Ninety percent of dealing was driving and sitting in the heat. Tweakers were never on time, but the long waits gave her private time with Graves.

"What happened with your paternity results?" she asked him.

Graves grabbed his hoodie and shook it to circulate the air. The air conditioner was blowing hot, as hot as the hundred-twenty-degree heat baking the car from the outside.

"No idea," he said after a minute.

"It's been a while," Erinn said, pointing her vent at him.

"I'm not Sadie's dad. They're not gonna waste time with me. All they want to do is find someone to foot the bill."

"Why do you always wear that hoodie?"

"Did you get tired of grilling me about Sadie and decide to pick on my wardrobe?"

Erinn wiped a tear away. "Whatever, it's not like I gave up everything to be a part of your life."

Graves unbuckled and shifted to face her. "You're acting crazy."

"I'm crazy?" Erinn gripped the steering wheel. "Who wears a hoodie in the summer?"

"Is that what you're upset about?"

"I'm not stupid," she said, staring at him. "You've been sneaking off with Lez and coming back high as fuck like you're possessed or some shit."

"So?"

"I want to see what you're hiding from see," she said.

Graves knew he'd been caught, and if he didn't strip down, the heat would kill him. He peeled the hoodie off his sweat-soaked shirt and shoved it behind the seat. On the crease of his arm, there were telltale black and blue marks that could have only come from a needle.

"It's infected," she said, averting her gaze.

Graves covered the swollen lumps with his hand. "You don't look so good either," he said, cutting back.

Erinn peeled her damp back off the seat. "Excuse me?"

A surge of pent-up emotion filled the air.

It wasn't all Graves' fault, but it felt like it was. Erinn knew she could've shared more with him, instead of hiding her pregnancy, the way he was hiding the needle. Maybe he would care more if he knew she was pregnant, but she needed him to want to get better on his own.

"Your face looks worse than my arm," Graves said, letting loose.

"It looks a million times better than your whore's face."

Graves couldn't help but laugh at the comment, and the laughter disarmed them both. Erinn chuckled reluctantly at first, then they both erupted. There were so many mixed emotions—pain, fear, anger, resentment, helplessness—all they could do was laugh.

"Lez is a hypocrite," Graves said. "Like, I'm forbidden from having sex with you."

"Are you serious?"

"She said it's okay for her to have sex with Fate, but it wouldn't be fair for me and you to hook up because I care about you too much."

A smile spread across Erinn's face, and her cheeks turned bright red. "If I'm off limits," she said with a wink. "Doesn't that like, make it sexier?"

She reached over and awkwardly put her hand on Graves' knee, teasing her way up.

"Sometimes I forget you're a virgin," he said.

"I'm not a virgin," Erinn said, smacking him. "You stole that from me."

Graves smiled. "We shared it."

Erinn moved her hand up, caressing him. "Jesus, are you hard already?"

"I've been hard since we left," he laughed.

She paused for a second, then climbed over the seat and straddled him, testing the limits of the cramped interior. Nothing like a little romance in the front of a Smart car. Graves pushed the passenger seat back as far as it would go to make room, then ripped his shirt off.

Erinn pulled her shirt over her head, feeling Graves' feverish skin press against hers. She moved rhythmically on his lap as their lips met. He slipped his hand under her skirt and then slid her panties aside.

A minute later, his pants were down and his dick was pressed between her legs. She gripped his shaft, smacking the tip against her pussy until they were both dripping with anticipation. Graves grabbed her hair and sank his teeth into her exposed neck, savoring the salty taste of her flesh as he pushed inside.

# Bitch Broth

## Graves

I can't believe I fucked Erinn. That's all I could think about the entire drive back to Scottsdale. There'd been no time to shower. Sweat had hardened around my body, and Erinn's discharge was dried on my dick.

"You should smoke some H or something," I told Lez when we got inside. "It'd be good to wind down."

"You hate when I smoke H."

I took my shirt off and tossed it onto the dirty laundry pile on the floor next to the bed, unsure what to say.

Lez crawled to the edge of the bed, her eyes fixed on me. Of all the sexless nights she'd smoked heroin and passed out... I pulled my jeans down slowly, like Erinn's pussy was just going to fall out and give everything away.

"I was thinking about you today," Lez said with a smirk.

"Oh yeah?"

"Yeah, while you were out. I'm not sure I like this new setup," she said. "You spending so much time with Erinn."

"Well, it's the only way."

Lez rolled onto her back, with her arms extended towards me. Her voice was low and slow, like she was moaning out the words as she spoke them.

"I was a bad girl today," she said, peeling her jeans off and tossing them aside.

My body betrayed me. I felt the swell as blood rushed to my dick. I didn't know what it was about that girl, but something ignited a fire in me. It wasn't the type of attraction I had to Erinn.

It was animalistic, feral even. I'm sure the meth had a lot to do with that, but I couldn't give in to temptation now.

"Are you seriously walking away?" Lez asked.

"I need to shower. It was hot out today, and I smell like ball soup."

"Like that ever stopped you before." Lez slid off the bed, her hand finding my dick as she stopped me before the bathroom. She dropped to her knees, wrapped her lips around it, then stared up at me with a crazy look in her eyes.

"You good?" I asked.

"I'm fine," she said. "Just curious why I'm eating Erinn's nasty pussy off your dick."

"It's not pussy," I told her. "It was hot out."

"I know what ball soup tastes like," Lez said, spitting Erinn's crusties onto the carpet. "That wasn't ball soup, it was bitch broth."

She hit my nutsack like a speed bag and watched me double over. The blow caused a swift, searing wave that reached into my stomach. Each beat of my heart amplified the pain, making it spread further. I swallowed a heap of vomit, choking on the burn as I countered her.

"You're a fucking hypocrite."

"We've been over this," Lez said, dressing herself in the bedroom. "You know why it's not the same as Fate, and you know that bitch is off limits. That's why you're allowed to screw Ash."

"Well, that's not an option anymore, is it?"

"I need that H now," Lez said. "Bring me the foil and lighter from my purse."

I grabbed her purse off the couch and dug through it. The fact that she wanted heroin and hadn't tried to kill me were both good signs. But when I was searching for the aluminum foil, I found something else, a letter.

"When were you gonna tell me about this?" I asked.

"I don't know," she said, clearly aggravated. "You didn't even want to take the paternity test."

I tore open the envelope, and my heart stopped.

"Sadie's mine..." My heart beat again. "99.9 percent positive match."

"Not a hundred."

"Are you serious? You're gonna contest .1 percent with the government. Fucking shit, how the fuck did I let you convince me that she wasn't mine?"

"You saw the texts from Ryder."

"That just proves Eva was cheating on me, it doesn't have a goddamn thing to do with paternity."

Lez looked scared. "There's another one," she admitted, pointing at the purse.

The other letter was from the Maricopa County Court, and right at the top, in big bold letters, there was another punch in the nuts.

**Hearing to Establish Child Support**

"The court date's already passed," I said, holding up the notice.

"So?"

"That means I've been ordered to pay support, while I'm still banned from seeing my daughter, who's actually my daughter. Oh, and I'm a fucking meth dealer because that's what hanging out with you leads to. How the fuck did I get here? I'm never gonna get my kid back."

"It's not my fault," Lez said. "You're the one who took the test."

"The test isn't the problem."

"Get the lighter and foil, like I told you," she said, filled with newfound conviction, "and then get the fuck out of my apartment."

"What do you mean, get out?" I asked.

Lez cocked her head like she was talking to an idiot. "You cheated on me, dickhead. I don't care what the fuck you do now, but you're not gonna sleep in my bed tonight when I'm pissed. Why don't you call your dumb little slut, Erinn? I'm sure she'd love to have seconds."

I pulled into the school Erinn wanted to meet at. She was standing beneath a lone streetlight, with a purse at her side. I thought she would get in her car and lead me to her place, but she just stood there, her eyes fixed on me.

"What gives?" I asked.

"You might wanna kill the engine."

She shoved her hands in her pockets, flicked her head, and started walking through the empty lot.

I locked the Dethbox and followed her, shielding my mouth from the dust clouds she kicked up, wondering where she was taking me. Walking around a school at night was creepy. I wanted to get to wherever we were going and forget about the shit that happened with Lez.

"Why'd that slut kick you out?" Erinn asked without turning around.

"She hated the taste of your pussy."

Erinn paused like she was confused, then took off again without asking any clarifying questions. She was fast, determined, even though she was heading nowhere. The parking lot lights faded as we rounded the field and traveled downhill. Ahead, all I could see was the outline of some drainage tunnels.

"Seriously," I said. "Where the fuck are we going?"

"Somewhere we can smoke." Erinn pulled a flare out of her purse and ignited it. Bright red flames erupted from the tip, illuminating the dark tunnels.

She slipped through the bars, careful to avoid their sharp metal edges. I followed after her, scraping my side on the rusty bars.

"Figured you'd fit right through," she said. "You're skinnier than I am."

"Tweakers don't eat."

"They do if they wanna live." She held the flare up and walked deeper into the tunnel.

I didn't want to follow her, but the flare's light was being swallowed by the tunnel, and I couldn't relax knowing there were spiders and scorpions crawling through the shadows at my feet. Unless I was in the glow of Erinn's flare, none of them would be visible, so I chased after her, choking on the hazy red smoke.

"Did you eat the banana?" Erinn asked as she tossed the flare on the ground and sat.

"That thing is rotten, and it's at Lez's."

Erinn patted the ground next to her. "Course it is."

I kicked the ground to scare away the bugs, then I sat next to her. Her face was painted in the dancing red light. If I had to imagine hell, it would be that tunnel, tormenting echoes, red flames, and stinging insects.

Erinn unzipped her purse, revealing a pipe and a baggie of meth.

"I didn't realize you had your own pipe."

Erinn rolled her eyes at me. "Are you one of those people who think other people just stop existing when you're not around?"

"You've barely smoked lately. I thought you were quitting."

"I'm trying," she said. "It's hard."

"I feel like I'm the one holding you back."

Erinn latched onto that statement, and for the first time in a while she looked excited. "What if we stopped driving for Fate?" she asked. "We could hold each other accountable."

"Fate knows my address," I told her. "Lez's ex is dating the mother of my child... What happens if I run away? If I said no, I'd be putting my family in the line of fire. I'm trapped here."

"Your child," Erinn said. "You got the results?"

"I just found out, and I don't know how to process it."

She handed me the pipe and shrugged, like she was feeling the same back and forth I was. Blinding moments of insight mixed with harsh reality. I lit the underside of the pipe, and as the crystal melted, it billowed like an apparition, reflecting the flare's light and casting an eerie red haze around Erinn. Her eyes were empty, unblinking, but reflective of our being.

"So," she said. "Do you even want to be a dad?"

Her comment caught me mid-smoke. "You handed me the pipe, though," I said. "Was I not supposed to take it?"

"I dunno."

"Look, if you don't wanna smoke, we can go to your place and pass out."

"You don't get it," she said. "This is my place."

I paused, struck by the sudden realization that I knew nothing about Erinn. Like where she lived, or who she lived with, or why she looked so wrecked lately.

"You don't sleep here..."

Erinn was straight-faced, eyes at the ground. "I sleep in the car. I hang out here."

"Why didn't you tell anyone?"

"Who would I tell?" she asked. "Would you have invited me to sleep on Lez's floor so I could watch you two fucking every night? No thank you. It's not like you really care, anyway."

"Don't you have anyone who can help?"

"Chels was the last person who was there for me." Erinn took the pipe back and stared at it like she hated the damn thing.

"What if we paid off your debt?" she asked. "Your family would be safe then."

"I'm not even allowed to see my daughter."

"Life gives us lots of chances," she said, pulling her crucifix pendant out from under her shirt. "I still believe that. Maybe there's a whole life you don't even know you could have, just waiting for you to open your eyes."

All I could muster was a shrug.

"You've already made your decision then. You don't want to be happy."

"I do want be happy," I said. "All the time."

"That's stupid," she said flatly. "No one is happy all the time. If people never felt bad, then feeling good wouldn't exist."

"I dunno, I've met people who look like they're always happy."

"Those people are content knowing they'll be happy again," Erinn said. "But you're a hedonist. Real happiness isn't about seeking or taking. It's about giving back and being there for the people you love."

"Well, thanks," I said. "Now I feel like shit."

"Good, that means you haven't forgotten how to feel. Which means you're still able to feel happy again, and maybe I can too."

The light from the flare dwindled. I knew there was more to Erinn's words, something she wasn't telling me, but I lacked the strength to pull it out of her. I got the basic point. She wanted more out of life. Both of us were trapped in this valley between our idealized dreams and the crushing reality of addiction.

"Do you think Lez and Fate ever feel this hopeless?" I asked her.

"I don't think they feel anything," she answered.

The light flickered out, taking our conversation with it. Nothing but questions, doubts, and fears lingered in the tunnel. We stayed there in the dark, huddled together, succumbing to the fear that this was life, and there was no way out. The uncertainty of tomorrow, our only constant.

Fate's apartment was a welcome reprieve from the tunnel. I held the door for Erinn, and we took our seats in the circle. The weight of the crew's gaze, Angel, Sam, and Zack, rested on us. No doubt Lez, who was absent from the circle, had given them a rundown of last night's blowout.

"Surprised to see us?" Erinn asked.

Zack chuckled. "I'd be surprised if we didn't, everyone comes back."

"Ash never came back," Angel said.

Zack glared at Angel, then cast his gaze at me. "Most people never leave."

That might've been the first time something Zack said made me think. It didn't matter what happened between the crew. Be it cheating, fighting, or even disposing of a body. Once the grip of meth took hold, you were destined to be with the only people who welcomed you. We came back because there was nowhere better to go. There were only worse places to go.

"Wonder where Lez and Fate are?" Erinn asked rhetorically.

Lez's moan pierced the bedroom door, as if on cue. Then the sharp smack of her flesh being pounded echoed through the hall. It's like they were waiting for me and Erinn to arrive, just to rub it in.

"Is that her big revenge?" I asked. "Like she hasn't been fucking Fate since day one."

Zack handed me the pipe. "Knowing doesn't make it hurt less."

I felt a twinge of discomfort, like Zack was letting me know he knew about me and Ash hooking up. He must've. But ignoring shit was the status quo. I offered the pipe to Erinn first, but she declined, so I lit that shit up hard and inhaled the intoxicating smoke, feeling pings throughout my body.

"It's time you got out of driving," I said to Erinn. "The cops haven't shown up."

"Are you coming with me?" she asked.

The slapping intensified, echoing throughout the apartment. Lez's moans were now a loud, exaggerated performance as she came on Fate's dick, while I nursed a bite on my arm.

"You'll get used to those," Erinn said, looking at my arm. "Like little needles."

All I did was get used to shit. I got used to this life, and used to these deals, and these people. Don't question it. Don't bother wanting more. This is what you get. Be happy with it. Nothing was ever resolved or dealt with. Things just kept eroding us, bit by bit, until we were tired, and angry, and bitter about keeping on.

"Oh good," Lez said, strutting out of Fate's room. "You're both here."

"You knew we were," I said.

"I made some calls," she replied. "Miguel had a little setback with his ecstasy supply. Which means we can upsell our pills to one of his clients."

"What pills?" I asked. I hadn't heard or thought about Miguel in ages.

"Are you fucking retarded? The pills you sold us when you first showed up here. We've been sitting on them until they were useful to us. Minus a couple that I took here and there."

"Why does it sound like you're part of Fate's business now?"

"Anyway," Lez said. "I was talking to Fate. If you and Erinn want to drive the deal and not fuck it up, then you and Fate are square. We keep the cash, and you can get the fuck out."

Erinn and I exchanged glances. It didn't feel real. Last night was a desperate surrender to a fate we couldn't control. Now we had a way out, and the first question that went through my mind wasn't 'how am I going to get Sadie back?' it was, 'who am I going to get meth from?'

"I'm not ready for this," I said, terrified at the thought of being sober.

Erinn slapped the back of my head. "Don't listen to him. We're so ready for this."

"Don't tell me the client is Skel."

Lez shook her head. "One of Miguel's regulars."

"As if that's better," I said, running through the outcomes in my head. "You want me to poach Miguel's client, someone who used to fuck Backslash, the girl who pointed the cops in our direction."

"That's how it works, Graves." Lez crossed her arms. "This wasn't easy to set up, you know. But I saw the stupid look in your eyes. If you want to be a dad so bad, then go be one."

Was this really happening, I wondered. Lez was being compassionate, and I was being a stubborn asshole.

"What if I say no?" I asked.

Fate walked out of his room in time to answer my question.

"It's not a choice," he said. "You're going on the deal, Erinn's driving."

Erinn drove while I kept my eyes out for Officer Hallman's Charger, or any other police cruiser for that matter. I knew she was excited, but we'd come too far to go down for dumb shit like speeding in a Smart car.

Nothing could go wrong. We had one shot. If it worked, then I had a chance of being a dad next year.

"Relax," Erinn said. "You're so tense right now."

"I've never met this guy before. We've never been to his hood. There's too many things I don't know."

"Don't worry." She looked over at me and smiled, her eyes crinkling at the corners like they had the first night we met. "This is the last bullshit deal we'll ever have to go on."

"Can we get some weed after?" I joked.

Erinn playfully narrowed her eyes, then slowed down. "This is the turn, right?"

I double-checked the printout and nodded. She turned into the neighborhood, and we rolled to a stop in front of house number 1602. A minute later we were greeted at the door by a guy in a tan flannel shirt, buttoned at the collar, with a wife-beater underneath and a pistol tucked in his belt.

"Graves?" the guy asked.

"That's me." I held out my hand. "Nico?"

Nico grunted in the affirmative and stared at my hand until I put it down, then nodded for us to follow him inside. There was an older couple on the couch in the living room. They didn't look related. They were just strung out and out of place.

We followed Nico up a narrow staircase that emptied into a small loft and led into a bedroom. Inside the bedroom was a group of people who looked scarier than Fate's crew.

I kept my hands tucked in my hoodie pocket. As my pulse quickened, sweat gathered on the bag of pills.

"Which of you has the money?" I asked, steadying my breath.

"Nah dawg." Nico looked at me like I was crazy. "You're driving us to the deal."

"That wasn't the plan."

Nico lifted the shirt flap over his gun. "Lez said you'd be cool with it."

Erinn shifted. Her shoulder pushed against mine as she moved closer. I stepped back and glanced around the room. These weren't the type of people who dropped ecstasy. Those people were fun, colorful, and living the P.L.U.R. life. This crew was solemn, quiet, and dirty.

"You realize we came here in a Smart car, right?" I asked.

"Then it's just me and you, Homie," Nico grinned from ear to ear. "Your girl stays here."

"I'm not leaving her."

Two of the guys in the room stood up and cracked their knuckles. Nico motioned for them to sit down and locked eyes with me. "I wasn't asking permission. The bitch stays put."

Erinn exhaled. "It's fine," she said, handing me the keys to her car. "Just make it quick."

I stood paralyzed between what I wanted to do and what needed to happen. We were unarmed, outnumbered, and at their mercy.

Nico guided me out of the room, his hand on my shoulder as he pushed me past the odd couple in the living room and through the front door. I took a minute to adjust the mirrors in Erinn's car before taking off.

"Nothing better happen to her," I said.

Nico chuckled at me. "You're kinda stupid, huh?"

That was the last thing he said to me. I drove that dick, his loaded gun, and hundreds of hits of ecstasy in silence, at the exact speed limit. My eyes studied every light and traffic fluctuation. I picked out cops and made sure I didn't draw any attention to us. But when a white dude in a Smart car drives through Guadalupe, there's no good way to be discrete.

At Nico's direction, I pulled up to an old house. Its defining features, warped panels with gaps on the side and no number. And like so many of the junkie houses I had been to, the weeds had overtaken the lawn.

"Wait here," Nico ordered. "I gotta make sure he's ready."

"What does that even mean?"

Nico shook his head as he got out. "It means fucking wait, pendejo."

As Nico made his way to the house, I pulled out my phone. I could only imagine Erinn's experience had been just as unpleasant as mine. I texted her to see how she was doing, then I turned my attention to my surroundings. No one was out, the streets were quiet aside from the strays, and the only thing I could hear was the quiet hum of the Smart car's small engine.

Erinn pressed her back against the cracked drywall. Since Graves and Nico left, conversation had been sparse, and she wanted to disappear. The pleasantries, the empty smiles, and the feigned interest all left a bad taste in her mouth.

"Hey, come sit with me," one of the guys said, motioning towards the mattress.

Her lips scrunched at the thought of sitting next to him, let alone on the dirty mattress. Even the girls were strange. Something was wrong with all of them. They looked like hyenas waiting to pounce.

"I'm gonna take a walk around the neighborhood," Erinn said.

She hurried down the stairs, but when she reached the landing, the older couple from the couch were blocking the doorway. "We can't let you leave," the old man said, placing his hand on the door.

Erinn looked at the woman beside him, who was as unwavering as the man. Then she heard footsteps coming down the stairs behind her. Her arms twitched, making her fingers jerk as the breath caught in her throat. The people were closing in. There was nowhere to run.

They hauled her back up the stairs, tossed her on the mattress, locked the bedroom door, and surrounded her. She tried to stand, but they shoved her back down on the bed.

"Stay there, beautiful," the old man said.

"Please," Erinn cried, curling up against the wall. "I don't want to be here."

The asshole reeled back and smacked her. "Disrespect," he muttered. "You're in our house, bitch."

Erinn clutched her face. It was hot and tingling. She could feel the outline of his fingers like fire. She tried to become as small as possible, tucking her head between her knees as the circle of junkies tightened around her. Hands slipped under her shirt. Her heart pumped harder, making her body shake with each pulse.

She kicked and flailed, panic rising. She couldn't break free. The room blurred and her mind retreated. Her clothes were ripped off as the crew violated her. When it was over, she was left trembling, her body broken, and her safety shattered.

Erinn called me, but her voice was muffled and frantic. I called her back, but she hung up midway through the first ring. Then I glanced at the time. Nico was still inside. The warped house was quiet, with no sign of movement.

I sent Erinn a text.

Everything good?

Another minute passed with no response and I was getting worried. The ecstasy was still in my pocket, and I didn't care if the deal was a bust, or if Nico had to walk his punk ass back from Guadalupe.

I shifted into drive, but just as I lifted my foot off the brake pedal, a Charger rounded the corner. The rearview mirror flickered with red and blue lights, and my heart stopped. I had hundreds of hits of ecstasy on me.

The telltale slanted headlights taunted me in the mirror. Officer Hallman stepped out, his shadow dancing off the pavement in the flashing lights.

"New ride?" he asked as I rolled down the window.

There was no point in lying. "Borrowed it from a friend."

"Shut off the engine."

I complied, silencing the low hum of the idling Smart car. I grabbed my wallet from my back pocket and handed my license to Hallman.

"Is there anything in the car I should know about?" he asked.

My heart pounded. I didn't know the law. Was he allowed to ask me that? What were my rights? Did it matter? The veins on my forehead felt like they were going to burst and stain the upholstery.

"Step out of the car for me," Hallman said.

I did, and as soon as I got out he told me to put my hands on the hood.

Again, I complied, pressing my hands on the hood while Hallman aimed his flashlight at the Smart car's interior. There wasn't much for him to scan in the tiny car. He looked under the front seat and then searched in the footwell.

He made his way to the passenger side next, cautiously patting the interior like he was expecting to get stuck with a needle. That wasn't standard protocol. Hallman knew this was a drug bust.

I pressed my eyes shut and held my breath. There was no escape, nowhere left to run. The only thing I could do was freeze while Hallman shifted his focus onto me and gave me a pat down.

# The Deal

The police station had a stale, office-like vibe. It looked more like Valley of the Sun Mortgage than I imagined a police station looking. Criminals weren't being shuffled around, and there were no frantic desk calls like in the movies. Everything was dull.

Hallman brought me into a small office. There was no two-way mirror either. Just him and me, seated on opposite sides of a wooden desk, with a water bottle sitting between us.

"Where do you want to start?" he asked.

I stared at my cuffed wrists. I wanted to go back to a time before any of this happened. A few months ago, I was just an ordinary guy, going through the motions. Now I was a strung-out criminal, haunted by demons. Everything happened so fast, but none of it felt quite so fucked until that moment.

"I'm not the person you think I am," I told Hallman.

"Is that so?"

"I have a daughter..."

Hallman looked concerned. "Where is your child now?"

"I haven't seen her in months."

That seemed to put Hallman at ease, knowing I wasn't around her.

"What can you tell me about Jennifer Woods?" he asked.

"Who?"

"I think you know who I'm talking about," Hallman said.

I'd never heard the name Jennifer Woods before, but I had to assume it was Jenna's full name based on Hallman's insistence.

Other than watching the poor girl die, I didn't know anything about her. Of course, he was probing about the death, and the decomposing body they pulled out of the trash.

All the thoughts that had been accumulating in my mind finally spilled over. Watching Jenna's eyes go blank, burying her body, losing my daughter, blocking the memory, using sex and drugs to dull the pain, rediscovering I was a dad just in time to push past the point of no return.

My head hung, and tears fell. "I wanted to tell someone, but I couldn't."

"Tell them what?"

"Fate made me hide her body," I said. "She overdosed. It wasn't anyone's fault, but he wouldn't let me leave. I had to help him."

Hallman continued to pull the story out of me. Jenna snorting heroin like it was coke, Fate's gun, the crew, and the drive to State Route 85 in the Dethbox where I helped dispose of her body. I hated recounting the details, but at the same time, I felt a weight lifting off me.

I told Hallman there was no one to blame, but that wasn't true. Jenna never would've died if there weren't drugs lying on the counter, or if this crew hadn't existed, or if she had real friends instead of addicts.

"You know," Hallman said. "When Backslash led me to your gang, I wasn't looking for a drug ring. I was investigating a suspicious death."

"How long were you watching us?"

"Long enough." Hallman's eyes shifted to the bag of ecstasy. "Do you realize what kind of prison time you're looking at?"

"A lot longer than I'd like."

"It sucks when the people you trust turn on you," Hallman said.

That comment stuck. "Who turned me out?"

"Well, I got an anonymous tip about this particular deal." Hallman sat back, stretching his arms. "She sounded frantic."

He identified the tipster's gender for a reason. He wanted me to know who it was, and to feel betrayed by them, so I could lead him further down the rabbit hole. My first instinct was to blame Lez, but she wouldn't sacrifice drugs or money just to screw me over. I had gotten a frantic and indecipherable call from Erinn though. And I don't know what happened at Nico's house, but she must've called the cops after trying to reach me.

"Is she okay?" I asked.

Hallman leaned forward and put both hands on the desk. "I don't know. She sounded like she was worried about you. So tell me, Ezekiel, where do we go from here?"

"What do you mean?" I asked.

"You're obviously a nobody. It sounds to me like you got yourself stuck in a world you don't want to be a part of, surrounded by people you don't like, doing things you hate doing."

"Kinda."

Hallman's gaze shifted and his posture softened. "Do you want to see your kid grow up?"

I nodded.

"Wait here," he said as he left the room.

As if I had any option other than waiting there, handcuffed to his desk. The walls felt like they were closing in on me, the cuffs tightening. That, or the pressure was making my wrists swell. Blood shot through my veins as my heart grew faster with each passing minute, and it didn't stop until Hallman threw the door open.

"You've got a chance to walk out of here," he said. "So listen up. This is how your deal is going to work..."

The second Hallman cut me loose, I headed to Nico's, only to find the place deserted. Fate's was next. Erinn's Smart car whined as I pushed its three-cylinder engine to the limit and hit the ramp into his parking lot.

Erinn was outside, hiding behind the Dethbox. I braked hard and skidded to a stop. She was alone, knees drawn into her chest, trembling.

"What happened?" I asked.

Erinn buried her face in her knees. "You just left me there."

"I'm sorry I didn't mean to ditch you."

I wanted to explain what had happened, but Hallman had warned me that my status as a confidential informant had to remain a secret. For my safety and for everyone else's.

"Look," I told her. "Some things went down that I can't get into right now. I couldn't get back any sooner."

"I guess that makes it all better," she snapped.

"Well, it's kinda your fault this happened, so maybe don't act shitty."

"Excuse me."

"You called the fucking cops on the deal. I get that you were freaking out, but what'd you think would happen?"

Erinn's eyes met mine as she raised her head. I'd never seen that look etched on her face—pure betrayal, hatred even. "I didn't call the cops," she sneered. "I called you, and you didn't come back for me."

The area under her eye was bruised and swollen.

"What the hell happened?" I asked.

"It doesn't matter."

"I tried to call you back, and I texted, but you didn't answer."

Erinn pulled her shattered phone out and threw it on the pavement.

"I couldn't bring myself to walk into Fate's," she said. "I've been waiting for you to get back. Did you get the money?"

"Cops broke up the deal, so there is no money."

"So... we're not leaving."

I couldn't tell her that I still had the ecstasy, or that I planned to work out another deal with it. Or that I was stuck in the life as an informant. Even if I made the money back, I wasn't able to ditch Fate's or bail out on Lez. All I could do was look at Erinn and shrug my shoulders.

"Things didn't go the way I hoped."

"They never do." She held her hand out. "Give me my keys."

"Come on, don't be like that. This isn't what I wanted. I had the worst fucking day, and the last thing I need is you taking it out on me."

"You had the worst fucking day?" Erinn got up and punched my shoulder. "I seriously can't believe how dense you are. You are the worst person I've ever met. You and Lez deserve each other."

"Seriously," I said. "Explain to me how I'm the worst person you've ever met?"

"You got me addicted to meth because you and your fucking friends were broke," she yelled. "Then you acted like you cared about me while you were busy fucking Lez. You strung me along even though you never planned to leave her and you never planned to stop selling drugs. I had plans for us, I had news to share with you, but you threw it all in the fucking trash."

"That's not fair."

"No, it's not fucking fair," she said through gritted teeth. "And I can't believe it took this happening to open my eyes. You act like you're this nice innocent guy, but you're not. You're just like everyone else in that circle of losers. You never wanted to leave them because this is your fucking home."

Under the flickering street light, I saw more than the bruises on her cheek. Her shirt had been torn. Makeup stains ran down her face and past the collar of her shit, and her shorts hung open where the button had been ripped off—there was blood smeared down her thigh.

"Seriously," I said, taking a step back. "What happened?"

"One of the million things that never should've happened to me. That never would've happened to me if I never met you. If I had listened to Chels, I would still be an actual person."

"I'm sorry that happened, but I didn't do anything to you."

"Well, you did actually." Her voice dropped low. "I know you were hurt and acting out. And from what you told me, your ex was a total bitch. But her being wrong doesn't make you right. And maybe you used to be a good person. But right here, right now, you're the bad guy."

"If I'm so bad, then why are you still here?"

"That's a great point," she said as she stepped into her car, and she didn't look back.

# Anger & Remorse

I pounded on Lez's door, having had a fifty-minute drive to wallow in Erinn's indictments, and deteriorate under the guilt of what I'd put her through.

Lez wouldn't want to see me, but I had to see her. I needed the pain to go away, and she had the needle.

She answered the door, naked and confused. "I didn't expect to see you."

There was a random guy tripping over his pants in the background. Seriously, she got rid of me the night before and already had a new fuck buddy staying over.

"Who is he, even?" I asked her.

"None of your business."

"Whatever," I said, collecting myself. "I need your help."

Lez crossed her arms, pushing her tits up as she scowled. "You're just gonna pretend you didn't get picked up today?"

"They didn't find the pills," I lied, realizing Nico must've reported back about the cops. The question was, how much did Nico see and what did he say? "Erinn's tags were expired," I said, giving Lez the cover story Hallman provided. "Her car got impounded, so it took time to drive back."

"How did you afford to get a car out of impound?"

"Uh... Erinn covered it."

"So, the bitch was holding out on us."

"It doesn't matter much now," I told Lez. "Erinn's gone for good. What I want to know is who called the cops in the first place."

Lez sassed her hips. "What the fuck are you looking at me for?"

"You and Fate set up the deal."

"I would never call the cops, you know that."

"Someone did," I said, pushing past her into the apartment.

"No shit." Lez slammed the door. "Backslash."

Meth makes you feel like you can't trust anyone. I'm not sure why I assumed Erinn or Lez had snitched on me, when Backslash was the obvious culprit. I was the only person who got grabbed while her contacts were clear.

"I'll deal with Backslash," I said. "But like I told you, I need help your tonight. You need to shoot me up."

"And Fate needs his pills back."

"I stashed them," I said. "Figured you weren't gonna hook me up unless you had to."

Lez looked like she was about to kill me, but I had the drugs, so I was in control. She got changed, grabbed her supplies, and came back with her fuck buddy in tow. I don't think he was a tweaker. He watched with morbid curiosity as Lez got the needle ready and then tied my arm off with the tourniquet.

"Clench your fist," she said.

I squeezed my hand—it was all going to disappear. The shitstorm that hurt Erinn and locked me in this life. The anger, the remorse, and the dwindling hope of reuniting with Sadie.

"What are you waiting for?" I asked her.

Lez plunged the needle in, depressing the plunger until the barrel was emptied. Chills encompassed me, hitting my spine like a lightning strike. My chest got heavy. I coughed. Then the sensation flipped. I went from ice-cold to sweltering hot so fast that I ripped my shirt off.

My heart stuttered. Thump... thump...

I clutched my chest. My heart had stopped beating. When it kicked in again, the shock sent me to the floor.

"Shit, that looked like a lot," the guy said.

"He's fine." Lez stood over me. "He's just being a bitch."

If I could move my mouth, I would've told them I wasn't fine. As my consciousness slipped away, the floor seemed to swallow me whole. Carpet fibers blurred and waved, like I was sinking underwater.

The bathroom looked impossibly far, but I clawed my way across the floor. Gripping the drawer handles as rungs, I hauled myself upright and faced the mirror.

All I could feel was the feverish surge through my veins. I splashed water onto my face. The shock snapped my vision back for a moment, but then my muscles seized, locking me in place before my own reflection.

A gaunt stranger stared back, eyes hollow and sunken. In that moment, I saw what Erinn saw, a lost and miserable junkie.

"This is how I die."

Lez glared at me in the mirror. "You're fine."

"I need food."

"We've got ketchup," her fuck buddy said. At least he was at least trying to be helpful. I heard the fridge door open and close, then the pantry. "There's no food. Just an old banana."

He ran back, clutching the black, shriveled fruit.

"Ew," Lez said. "Throw it away."

"No," I stammered, the word barely escaping.

He squeezed the rotten banana pulp into my mouth. The mush ran down my paralyzed throat, and it tasted like the sweetest nectar, and I swear it gave me the strength to carry on.

"Call 911," I choked.

"We can't call 911," Lez said. "You just slammed meth."

"Then take me to the fucking hospital."

If there was no one else present, she would've let me die. Instead, she agreed to drop me and my car off, and have her guy follow so he could drive her back. Together, they carried my stiff body to the Dethbox and forced me inside.

The world was a haze after that. Headlights streaked, lane lines blurred, and my mind drifted. Then, the tires screeched to a halt in front of the hospital.

Lez pulled me out of the Dethbox, then sped off. The lights dimmed, and my body got stiffer. I still didn't know what I believed, but in that moment I can tell you one thing: I fucking prayed—for forgiveness and mercy.

# Hypokalemia

I woke to the sterile white of the hospital room, brisk air, and an ache in my chest. A clear bag of fluid was suspended above me, with a thin tube snaking its way to my arm.

Sadie's voice echoed in my head. "Up, Daddy."

I'd nearly lost it all. I realized in that moment I could've given up that voice forever. I promised myself that given this second chance, I'd fight for her.

There was a knock at the door, and a man in a white coat walked in.

"I'm Dr. Patel," he said, stepping up to the bed. "How are you feeling today?"

"Like shit."

The doctor marked something on his chart and then, with a half-cocked smile, asked, "Why is that, do you think?"

"Probably the drugs."

Dr. Patel nodded. "What year is it?"

"2008."

"Good, and can you tell me your name?"

"Graves," I said, then reconsidered. Erinn was right. You don't just get to be happy all the time, but you can still experience it. The problem was that happiness couldn't come from a pill or a needle. It would need to come from *me*, not Graves, doing what *I* knew to be right. Only then could happiness become a part of my story. "My name, it's Zeke," I said. "Ezekiel."

Blinding moments of clarity may come to tweakers, but the revelation that came with facing death was a far more powerful experience. I didn't want to be Graves anymore. That a-hole started all this shit. He hurt Erinn and did things Zeke never would have. As far as I was concerned, Graves died that night, and if anyone was going to put things back the way they should be, it had to be the real me.

"Now for the important question," Dr. Patel said. "Was this on purpose?"

"Like... was I trying to kill myself?"

The doctor, pen poised above the chart, nodded expectantly, awaiting my reply. The answer, I knew, meant the difference between an involuntary hold in a psych ward and being released. Truth be told, I wasn't sure what I wanted when I asked Lez to shoot me up. Maybe I wanted an easy way out, but this wasn't the venue.

"It was just an accident," I said.

"Meth is a serious drug, Zeke." Dr. Patel put the chart down, removed his glasses, and looked me dead in the eye. "It's not just the drug. It's the lack of hygiene and malnutrition too. Without potassium, your heart cannot generate the electric signals that control rhythm."

"I couldn't even move."

"Hypokalemia-induced paralysis. If you went a second longer without potassium, you would not have made it through the night."

"No way." I shook my head in disbelief. "That stupid fucking banana."

Dr. Patel's brow furrowed. "You're sure you feel okay?"

It wasn't the right time to smile, but I couldn't help it. A grin slowly spread across my face. Erinn's gift gave me just enough juice to keep my heart ticking on the way to the hospital. For the last couple of months, I'd been faced with the signs and the warnings. Sure, the triple six license plates could've been a coincidence, but one thing was certain: that banana was a goddamn miracle.

"I think I have a guardian angel."

"It would appear so," Dr. Patel said. "Here," he added, jotting an address on scratch paper and handing it to me. "This is an excellent support group. The court sends people here for recovery, but anyone can attend. I've referred more than a few overdoses." Then, his tone shifted back to business. "Now that you're stable, someone will be in shortly to collect your insurance information and go over the paperwork."

The moment Dr. Patel left the room, I ripped the IV from my arm and found my clothes crumpled in a bag in the corner. All but my shirt, which I left at Lez's. I'd have to stop at Walmart and grab a T.

I slipped past the nurses and down the hall topless, and I didn't stop until I smelled the heat rising off the asphalt.

Lez had parked the Dethbox back in the lot. The keys were on the seat, but the glove box hung open—she found the pills.

My stomach lurched with a sudden, unsettling twist. What was I going to tell Officer Hallman? And with that discomfort, the cravings snuck in. Meth had become my default response to every uncomfortable feeling, my answer to every question. I pulled the support group's information from my pocket. Was I worthy of redemption... was I capable of it?

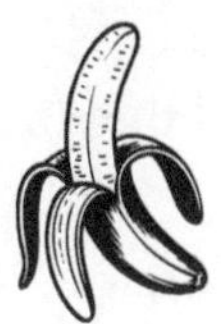

The support group met at a nondenominational church. Believe it or not, I didn't burst into flames when I walked through the door, but I did regret going. It's complicated to explain the addiction mentality.

I wanted help during the split second when I decided to go. Then I didn't think I needed it on the drive over. Towards the end of the drive the itch got so bad I almost detoured to Fate's, so I went to the church.

But if we're being honest, support felt like a load of shit.

"You're a new face," a guy said.

He introduced himself as Doug and led me to the coffee. It wasn't meth, but it would have to do. I looked at the sanctuary as I struggled to drink the stale brew. Chairs had been pushed into circles, which gave me a chuckle. Addicts sat in circles taking drugs, then sat in circles to quit.

Doug turned out to be the chairperson. "We've got a new friend," he said, parading me in front of the strangers.

I expected bikers and burnouts. Instead, I ended up sitting between an IT professional and a soccer mom. As a newbie, I got picked on by Doug to share first, but I told him I was only there to listen. The IT guy to my right started, and over the course of an hour, we circled around to soccer mom on my left.

"They tell you that time heals," she began. "It's been five years now, and I still set the table for my daughter."

Until that moment, I had decided that those people and I had nothing in common. But I felt a rush that whipped my head in her direction, and I kept my focus on her as she revealed the most horrifying story I had ever heard.

"I drank too much, and I passed out... I didn't hear her crying for help."

My eyes shifted around the circle, and I got the feeling that the worst had happened.

"The worst part is," she said. "No one blamed me."

The people clapped, offering their sympathy. I don't know what a person does when they lose a child forever and blame themselves. There was a feeling in me, like I wouldn't be able to go on after losing just one year with my kid, and here this lady was, fighting to regain her sanity.

There was a whole world of horror I hadn't even come close to facing, and when the circle came back to me, Doug asked me to share again. I kind of felt awful even thinking about complaining.

"I haven't seen my daughter since I started using," I stammered.

Doug leaned forward. "That sounds hard."

"I never used drugs around her, but when she got taken away from me, everything fell apart, and I started using."

"Those moments when things get tough are a true test of our willpower," Doug said. "I don't know the circumstances and I won't pry, but maybe being apart from your daughter is a blessing in disguise. When you have a kid, you are their rock. Your world can't fall apart."

"I want to be there now," I said. "But I'm trapped."

"We all feel trapped," Doug acknowledged. "It's a state of mind. There's no one forcing you to do anything. You are in control."

A few heads in the circle nodded, but mine shook. "This isn't metaphorical. I had to become an informant to avoid prison, but I lost the bait drugs and I'm freaking out."

"You can't bring a kid into a life like that," Doug said.

Why didn't I consider that?

It's like I was a child, throwing my life away for a buzz and thinking only about myself. Even when I thought about Sadie, it was in the context of me. How could Eva take her away from *me*? What did *I* do to deserve this?

The questions I needed to ask were: How was this going to affect Sadie, and what type of father did she deserve?

"I had a kid once," a gruff voice rumbled from another circle.

My eyes were drawn at once to the back of a man's bald head, and the telltale eyeball tattoo staring back at me—Three-Eyed John. He stood, flashing his Desert Vultures jacket before turning to face me.

"I thought I recognized that candy-ass voice," he said.

Doug stood. "Keep it calm, John."

"I got questions for you," John said, pointing at me. "The police so happened to knock on my door the night you were there."

"The cops arrested you for possession," Doug said. "Remember how we talked about accountability?"

John was fuming, his chest rising and falling. "My old lady left me," he said. "They took our son."

Doug kept trying to diffuse the situation. "Take five and breathe," he said. "No one here is perfect. We're working the program. Don't forget your plea deal hinges on my assessment."

John grunted as he lowered himself into his seat.

"Speaking of deals," Doug said, turning back to me. "What are the terms of your gig as a confidential informant?"

All I could do was look at him like a deer in headlights.

"How do you get out?" Doug asked.

At no point had Officer Hallman discussed terms. It's not something I'd considered until Doug mentioned it, and then it was the only thing I could think about. Had I traded Fate's hold over me with Hallman's?

Three-Eyed John chuckled from the adjacent circle. "You made a deal with the devil."

Doug clapped his hands together. "Break time."

The circle shot up from their chairs. Half of them headed for the coffee dispenser, and the other half hurried outside to smoke. I joined the coffee crew, and Doug snuck up behind me with a business card.

"You need a lawyer," he said. "This guy is good."

The card was thick and embossed with black lettering:

**Ronald Blake**

"Free consult," he said. "If you think life is hard now, wait until you have to turn on the people you call friends."

"I'm not looking forward to it."

Doug appeared sympathetic, while also being blunt. "It's you or them."

"Them." I knocked back the rest of my coffee, crushed the Styrofoam cup, and tossed it into a trash can. "I don't think I'm gonna come back, John kinda scares the shit out of me."

"You can still work the steps," Doug said.

"How?" I asked.

"Be accountable, and make amends, and no more stinkin' thinkin'."

I took his advice to the Dethbox and booked a consultation with Ronald Blake for the next day. If I wanted to do right by Sadie, then I needed to figure out my terms and get away from this crap. In the meantime, I figured I could pay Levi a visit and work on making amends.

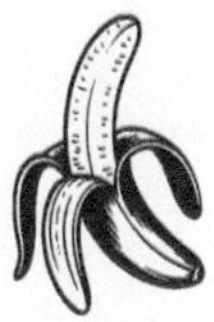

My nerves were fried. I swear a guy on a motorcycle tailed me to Levi's. Either that, or I was just paranoid about John and the Desert Vultures. The IV fluids from the hospital had leveled me out for a while, but the longer I spent sober, the less stable I felt.

Paranoid or not, I didn't want to wait around in the open while Levi took his sweet time to answer. I pounded until the door swung inwards, but he blocked me when I tried to step inside.

"What do you want?" he asked.

"Let me in," I said, checking behind me.

Levi looked past me. "Why?" he asked. "What'd you do?"

"People were following me... I think." The sun was beating down, and my skin was hot and crawling. "Come on."

He didn't move. Instead, he judged me. "I've been calling and texting you. You realize you bailed on me and left me to pay the rent by myself."

"That's kinda why I'm here."

"You look like you're drugged out of your mind," he said.

Cool air wafted out of the house, begging me to walk in. "I'm gonna meet with a lawyer like you wanted," I told him. "There's some steps I need to do, and I was hoping to stay here."

"You can't just throw your life away, ignore me, and then show up on my doorstep and ask for a place to crash."

I heard the aggressive roar of a motorcycle engine and jumped out of my skin. I tried to slip past Levi, but he shoved me and I landed hard on the pavement.

The amends had failed. Like Erinn, I had nowhere to sleep but my car.

# The Lawyer

After a burning hot sunrise in the Dethbox, the law offices of Beckerman and Blake offered a reprieve. Sweat evaporated in the brisk air, leaving a trail of salt behind. As I approached the receptionist's desk, I prayed her floral perfume would mask the stink coming from my pores.

"Ezekiel?" she asked, her voice flat as she typed.

I'd almost forgotten what real people smelled like, let alone looked like. The woman's nose instinctively wrinkled when her gaze lifted from the computer. She scrutinized me from head to toe as she stood.

"Follow me," she said, adjusting her skirt.

Her suit jacket was pressed, stain-free, and seemed to hold her straightened hair with its prominent shoulder pads.

It'd been a while since I'd cared about what I looked like, but her presence made me fixate—soot stains from the pipe, dirt, and grime. I didn't know when I'd showered last, but I was acutely aware that it was not recently.

"Mr. Blake will be with you in a moment," she said as she left.

I faced my reflection in the window, fixed my hair, and rubbed my eyes.

Ronald Blake walked through the door the second the clock on the wall struck nine. "You get thirty minutes," he told me. "You mentioned two issues on the phone: a recent arrest and custody of a minor child."

I had to be quick, but I couldn't afford to overlook any details. "I'm stuck in a C.I. deal," I said. "I need to get out so I can get my kid back."

"Take a seat, please," Ronald said as he sat behind the desk.

I sank into the boxy wooden chair and tried to catch my breath. That day marked my second day of sobriety. My hands were shaking, and it didn't help that my heart was racing as I revisited the trauma.

"Take me back to the start," he said. "How did you lose your child?"

"I was just trying to be there..."

With a couple of minutes already gone, I quickly summarized the events at a speed I hoped he could understand. I used to be a decent guy, a parent who was unfairly separated from his daughter. I explained the order of protection and how that led to my addiction, as well as the paternity test and missed court dates.

"You never used drugs around your child?" Ronald asked.

"Never."

Ronald sat back in his chair and shook his head. "There's a lot to unpack here, but I have to ask, why didn't you contest the order of protection in the first place?"

"It's expensive, and I didn't think anyone would believe me."

"Lucky for you, the burden of proof lies with the accuser. If there was no damage done, no police involvement, no verifiable injuries sustained, hospital visits, etcetera, then there's no hard evidence of wrongdoing. It's odd that you've waited this long, but we can still contest the order in court."

"Really?"

"You mentioned Eva texted you after the order. She violated her own terms of non-contact. I don't think she would face any consequences, especially at this stage, but that shows she clearly isn't afraid of you."

"So if we win, I could see my daughter again?"

Ronald offered a half-smile. "Let's talk about your parental rights, or lack thereof. Unwed fathers have no implied rights. While your ex is entitled to support, you're not entitled to parenting time or legal decision-making."

I leaned forward in my seat. "How does being wed determine fatherhood?"

"It shouldn't," he said. "But it does. We need to get the order quashed first, and then we can fight the next battle."

"So we're talking two court cases, and then maybe I can see her?"

"That's not the hardest part. To get any rights, you'll need to convince a judge that you can hold a job, provide a stable residence, and maintain sobriety."

"Eva just gets to be a mom regardless of personal circumstances, make up lies that I need to contest, and then the court scrutinizes everything I do for whatever rights they decide to give me?"

"Bingo... and none of it matters if you're working as an informant. For your daughter's safety, you need to get away from that life."

The slight glimmer of hope I had was gone. To think, all of this could've been avoided if I'd just listened to Levi, gone to the damn consultation, and had his stupid garage sale to raise cash.

"What are the terms of your C.I. deal?" Ronald asked.

I buried my face in my hands, then dragged them through my hair, feeling the strands snap between my fingers.

Ronald glanced at his watch, the thirty-minute mark was approaching. "You'll need to figure that out," he said.

"What should I do?" I asked. "In brief."

"Demand terms from Officer Hallman, get them in writing and get it signed. Offer him something to sweeten the pot. I'm sure there's someone you know who should be arrested."

I nodded. Backslash screwed me. She was going down, and her bust was gonna pay for my filing. I texted Hallman to get the ball rolling, I just needed to get those pills back.

"Then file to contest the order of protection and establish parenting time and decision making," Ronald continued. "I recommend having representation, but if you can't afford that, you can at least hire our firm to file."

"Okay." I looked at my phone clock, thirty seconds. "What then?"

"A hearing to contest the order will be scheduled within ten business days of request. Parenting time and legal decision-making can take longer to process. You need to establish the requirements we talked about for parenting time and legal decision making to work out."

"I need to make some money. I'll be back to file."

"Once we file," Ronald warned. "The countdown begins. Be ready."

Ready meant maintaining more than two days of sobriety, landing a job, and having a stable residence. Sobriety, as painful as it was, was underway, but sleeping in the Dethbox wasn't a viable option. I'd need to have another conversation with Levi, just as soon as I got the pills back from Lez.

# The Pills

"I thought you were dead," Lez said, staring at me from the doorway.

The air wafting from her apartment was thick with heroin. Molecules stuck like peanut butter in my throat. I may hate heroin, but I couldn't have asked for better luck when it came to negotiating with Lez.

I pushed past her into the apartment. "Thanks for caring."

"Where've you been?" she asked.

"Involuntary hold," I lied. "The hospital thought I tried to kill myself, so they put me on suicide watch."

"And what are you doing at my apartment?" she asked, sassing her hips.

"You took my pills."

She shut the door so the neighbors wouldn't hear her raise her voice. "They were never your pills."

If there's one thing I'd learned about tweakers, it's that they're opportunistic. I opened her kitchen drawers, checking for the ecstasy. "Did you keep them or give them to Fate?" I asked. "Because Slash wants to buy them back."

After a minute of processing, Lez shook her head. "You're not gonna sell to that bitch."

"So, you do have them then."

Lez walked past the kitchen into the bedroom, but instead of grabbing the pills, she pulled out Spin-derella. "I know for a fact you haven't smoked," she said. "Are you going straight like Erinn?"

"I'm trying to cut back considering what happened."

"You got picked up," she said, loading the bowl. "Now you want to sell my pills to the bitch who called the cops... there's no way in hell I'm trusting you until I see you smoke this."

I was standing at a crossroads, torn between sobriety and getting Hallman his bust. Every instinct told me to get out and find another way—there was none. In a way, smoking meth was for Sadie. At least that's what I told myself.

Lez handed me the pipe. My chest tightened, breaths coming in shallow bursts. Three days, I told myself. Three days and it would be out of my system.

"That's a good boy," she said.

I didn't want it to feel as good as it did. It shouldn't have been able to comfort me, not after everything I'd been through. Despite all I'd learned and overcome, relief crept in anyway, and that made it hurt even more.

I sat on the bed, defeated, and Lez sat beside me. She must've been bored, or horny from the heroin, because the next thing I knew I felt the warmth of her breath on my neck as she unbuttoned my pants.

It was automatic for her, and as my dick stood at attention, I realized it was automatic for me too.

"You think this deal is gonna work?" she asked, stroking me.

"Backslash won't tank her own deal."

"I'm not letting you out of my sight," she whispered. "I don't trust you."

The agony dissolved as she touched me, while I felt the rush of meth coursing through my veins. Erotic pleasure and gratification blossomed, supplanting grief and responsibility. I shoved her face down on the mattress and ripped her pants off. It was a weird dynamic we had. I hated her just as much as she hated me, and I wanted to pump that hate deep inside her.

"You're taking me on the deal," she moaned, clenching her pussy.

"I can handle Backslash," I said as I pushed her head down into the mattress. "I don't need a fucking babysitter."

Her hands pushed back against my lower abdomen. She was trying to cushion the impact. "Fuck me as hard as you want," she said, holding back whimpers. "You're not selling those pills without me."

I stopped pushing her head down long enough to land a hard slap on her ass. Her legs gave out and I lay down on her, whispering, "I hate you," as I pumped her pussy full of cum.

And that's how quickly everything you've worked for can slip away. Just one slut and some drugs you can't resist. I pulled out and slapped her ass again, still wondering why either of us would do any of the things we did.

Then I rolled onto my side and texted Hallman.

We have a problem.

Were you able to set up the deal?

Yeah, but this girl is attached to the pills, I can't get wired beforehand.

Same time and place we discussed… Call me when you make the deal, and I'll record the line.

# Bringing Down Backslash

I smoked that morning after spending the night with Lez. It's the only way I could force myself to go through with the deal. The flood of mixed emotions inside me brought tears to my eyes, which I quickly wiped away.

"Fucking dust," I said, readjusting the cabin air vent.

"Is that biker still behind us?" Lez asked, glancing in the side mirror.

I was beginning to worry that I wasn't just paranoid. That Three-Eyed John was tailing me, and that I was going to have a run-in with the Desert Vultures soon. My only hope was that they would get themselves in trouble with Hallman.

"Let's talk cash," I said, changing the subject. "I need a couple hundred."

"Or not," Lez said.

"I need to go to court for Sadie. Remember all those letters you hid from me."

"The deal was Fate gets the money, you get out."

"But you thought I was dead."

"Now I know you're not," she said, scowling at me. "If you want to be square with Fate, then this money goes to us."

Getting out from under Fate's thumb was still essential, so I didn't push, even if it set my timeline back.

I reached into my pocket, texting Hallman by muscle memory.

We're almost there.

The biker was still following, but when I turned down Backslash's street, he rode past. I breathed a sigh of relief as the roar of his engine faded. Now I could focus on the important thing, giving Backslash a taste of her own medicine. I pulled over next to the call box, rolled down the window, and punched in the gate code.

**6-8-3-2**

Backslash's voice crackled over the speaker. "Graves?"

"I told you it's Zeke now."

"Whatever."

The box beeped, and the rusted chains ahead of us sprung to life, retracting the gate.

Lez looked at me as I revved the engine and pulled through.

"You're going by Zeke, huh," she said.

She was giving me that look again. The same guarded stare she'd given me yesterday, like she was waiting for me to turn on her. I could see the distrust in her eyes, but I was sure it would fade when she got her money.

As I steered into the parking lot behind the complex, there was a nagging voice in the back of my head: Backslash was your friend. The thought stung. It sounded ridiculous, but it was true. Backslash was the closest thing I'd had to a real friend in years, besides Damien.

The rest of the crew? They were just there. Lez was, well, she was Lez, and Erinn hated me now.

I passed by Hallman's Charger, and my heart kicked into gear. It was real. There was no turning back now. I led Lez across the brittle grass toward Backslash's place, retracing the path Damien had shown me when this all began. Everything was the same, but it felt different now—emptier.

I remembered the first time I saw Backslash in that black club dress, and how she felt so untouchable and awesome. And how badly I wanted to be a part of her world back then. Now, all I wanted was to escape. To forget that any of this had ever happened. The weight of what I was about to do pressed down on me as I hit the call button in my pocket, giving Hallman ears.

Backslash met us outside, wearing that same slutty black dress.

"Well, isn't this some shit," she said.

"Buying back your own drugs for more than they're worth," Lez snipped. "Sucks to be dry. Guess being the cartel slut isn't working out for you."

"It just sucks I have to look at your face," Backslash shot back. "Take the money and go."

"It's forty-three eighty-nine," Lez said.

Backslash looked at me. "That's not the price I talked about with Zeke."

"Well, that's what it is," Lez told her.

I didn't need to lead the conversation. Lez was giving Hallman everything he needed, and she was being so loud there was no doubt he could hear over the phone.

Backslash turned her gaze at me after she agreed to Lez's upsell. "I expect this kind of shit from her, but I thought you were better than that... You're gonna charge me seven a pill after everything we've been through?"

"You turned on me," I said, feeling a surge of adrenaline.

Then Backslash went and did the one thing I never expected of her. She looked me in the eye and said, "I'm sorry," as she handed the money to Lez.

A knot twisted in my stomach.

Lez had just squeezed Backslash for more than the deal was worth, and she wasn't even going to give me what I needed for Sadie. Meanwhile, I just condemned the only person here who'd ever offered me a shred of decency. She apologized, and I was about to repay her with a prison sentence.

It felt like crossing a line that I could never come back from.

Lez saw me freeze, so she grabbed my arm and pulled me back towards the Dethbox.

"Great," she said. "You're sorry. She's sorry. Everyone's sorry. We don't need to talk about our feelings."

"I wish you'd picked me over them," Backslash called after us.

I didn't have the heart to answer her or even turn around. Instead, I pretended the comment didn't sting as I walked away, that it didn't make leaving nearly impossible. Why the fuck did she have to apologize and say nice things and act like we were still friends?

I hung up on Hallman so I could text Backslash.

For real though, I'm sorry.

Hallman's Charger crept closer as Lez and I got into the Dethbox. Lez saw it and shot a look at me. "Let's go," she said. Little did she know that we were in the clear. We pulled out and navigated down the apartment road as Hallman and his partner moved in on Backslash.

I dropped Lez off in Scottsdale and drove back to the police station. If that bust moved their investigation to the right people, freedom was within my reach. I hurried to the counter and asked the receptionist to call Hallman.

It took an hour for him to come get me, giving me plenty of time to sit and ruminate on the situation. I kept checking my phone, hoping Backslash would respond to my texts, even though I knew she couldn't.

When Hallman sat me down in his office, my throat tightened, and I struggled to hold back the tears.

"You did good," he said. "That was a clean bust, the first of many."

"Can we use the pills again?" I asked.

Hallman's gaze lingered on me, like I was an idiot. "That's material evidence, Zeke."

"Yeah, but I wasn't able to keep the money, and I really need it to file paperwork for my daughter's custody case. And if I can use the pills again, then I can set up another deal, and we can—"

Hallman dropped a bulky folder onto the desk with a thud. "This isn't you setting up deals to make money. These are police investigations. You can't request evidence back from me, period."

I had to sit with that thought and really let it sink in. Selling the same drugs over and over made sense to me. I could avoid meth, and I could avoid Fate. But not anymore, I would need Fate and his meth to help Hallman.

"I took down a friend," I said, burying my face in my hands. "What's gonna happen to Backslash, like, what kind of charges is she looking at?"

"Possession with intent to distribute, for starters." Hallman sat across from me, his eyes devoid of emotion. "With priors, she's looking at five to ten years at a minimum, unless she has worthwhile information to offer us. Nothing is set, Zeke. Everything is a bargain here."

I hoped she'd turn on Miguel. He was an asshole anyway. But the fact that I put her in that situation, and didn't even get what I needed from it, felt pretty damn awful. Ecstasy wasn't a means to unlimited pleasure or a way to make money. Those pills were a one-way ticket to misfortune.

"Let's talk terms," I told Hallman. "I just delivered someone who can give you names of cartel members and drug traffickers."

Hallman squinted, like he was having a hard time considering my position. "Look," he said after a minute. "I get that you want to see your kid, but we're invested in you. I can't just throw you back without getting help." Then his gaze softened a bit. "I'll cover your damn filing fees, but I need you out there."

"But once I file, I'm going to have a court case within like ten days."

"Not my problem."

"And whenever the next case happens, I could have custody of my daughter again."

Hallman laughed at me. "No one's giving you custody of a minor. You'll be luck to get supervised visitation on the weekends."

"Maybe more if I can show the court I'm in a good place."

"Let me be very clear with you, Zeke. You are in a bad place. And you will not be in a good place any time soon. My advice to you is take my help, get the paperwork filed, and see your kid for a couple of hours a month."

"Fine," I said, crossing my arms.

"You look like hell," he added. "Take a week off and figure things out. Try to find a place you can stay without getting high and treat this like a job. Clock in, bam, you're a dope fiend. Clock out, boom, father."

As if it were that simple.

"I'm gonna call my lawyer," I told him. "Let's take care of the filing now. I'll just use my brother's address on the paperwork."

My mind was already planning out who I could take down next. Fate was my first choice, but I needed his business. Billy's drug den, on the other hand, was ripe for the taking. In the meantime, maybe I could give things with Levi another shot, making amends and shit.

# Amends

I idled outside Levi's place, rehearsing an apology in the rearview mirror. I went in too hot last time. Literally and figuratively. And while I couldn't do a thing about the sweltering weather, I could temper my attitude.

"I'm sorry I bailed on you," I said aloud. "There's a lot of feelings inside me that'd built up for way too long. I'm pissed off that Dad was never around, and that Mom was taken from us, and it feels like we never had a chance."

For some reason, the practice apology was working me up. I took a moment to collect myself before returning my gaze to the mirror. In that moment, I wasn't the husk I'd seen on the night of my overdose. There was a human being staring back at me. Someone who'd been trapped deep inside.

"I've been scared, and even when you were around, I felt alone. Being a father, it was supposed to be a beautiful thing that came with a family, and instead it became another thing that was never going to work the way it was supposed to. Because someone was fighting me every step of the way."

At that point I was in tears, my body desperately trying to release the cortisol welling up inside. I wiped my face and went to the door. Levi knew I'd been crying. My face was puffy and my eyes were bloodshot. And honestly, I don't know how much of what I rehearsed made it out of my mouth before he gave me a hug.

I guess all he wanted was an apology. He led me inside.

All the insurmountable problems I thought I had when I lived there seemed minuscule now. Even losing Sadie, the most crushing blow I'd ever suffered, would have been a walk in the park compared to my current situation.

Levi grabbed a pizza from the fridge and put out two plates. "You understand that you need to eat to live, right?"

"Yeah, I get that now," I snickered.

Levi watched me eat, then asked, "Where's your necklace?"

"Does it matter?" I asked him. "It's not like I believe in anything, anyway."

"That's not true," he said. "You've never believed in the literal sense. The Bible is made of stories though, and you've always been good at understanding meaning, even if you suck at emulating good behavior."

"That sounds like a dig."

"Kinda," he laughed. "But you've always believed in something greater than yourself, even if you don't know what it is."

"Yeah, well, there are lots of things greater than me."

He didn't push on the necklace. I think he knew what it meant to me and assumed I'd sold it for drugs. That memory of our mother was gone forever.

"So, what's your plan?" Levi asked.

"I was hoping to find a stable residence," I told him.

"I don't know if you've noticed, but everything is gone," he said, looking around. "The market crashed, our rent is through the roof, and I had to sell just about everything to make payments without you."

"Did you sell my computer?" I asked.

Levi side-eyed me. "Not yet."

"I'll start sending out resumes tonight, and we'll get the bills under control."

I knew I couldn't hide being a confidential informant, so I filled Levi in on the details and promised not to bring anyone around the house, under penalty of getting kicked the fuck out.

Then I stepped into my old room, a place I never thought I'd miss, and collapsed on the bed. I had seven days to detox and get my head straight before I had to contact Hallman.

# The Seventh Day

On the seventh day, I found myself back at the park where Sadie and I used to play, allowing the fresh air to fill my lungs. The week leading up to that moment had been a battle. The first day, exhaustion hit me like a freight train. Every sleepless night caught up, but in a way, I was thankful. Sleep kept the cravings at bay.

The second day, hunger took hold. I raided the fridge and ate all of Levi's food. He was pissed, and I was sick, but my body needed to replenish the nutrients I'd been depriving it of. I spent the rest of that day lying in bed, sending out applications online while I tried to digest.

By the third day, fatigue and hunger had faded, replaced by unshakable depression. The world outside looked gray, and sunshine felt like a lie. I punched a hole in the wall just to feel something. That darkness bled into the next day—cravings, anger, resentment. I almost relapsed, but before I got the nerve to leave the house, Levi delivered a letter. The court had scheduled my hearing to contest Eva's order of protection. It gave me a reason to keep going.

I called Hallman and postponed our next bust, Billy's drug-den, until after the hearing. The pressure of court and the weight of it all turned the fifth night into a vivid and debilitating nightmare.

Then day six hit, and the worst of the torment had passed. My body was twitching, but I could breathe. I spent the day in meditation, letting my mind search for peace.

And so there I was, on the seventh day, under the shade of a non-native Aleppo pine tree in the park where my last real memory of Sadie was, just thinking. And I realized for the first time that the park wasn't fake at all. The pine had been transplanted from somewhere else, but it was still a real tree, providing real shelter. It had been transplanted to make something as empty and inhospitable as the Arizona desert livable.

Sometimes life can feel barren and empty like the desert. We're not always given the perfect environment, and it's up to us to transplant love and compassion. To fill the void with our own meaning.

Creating something beautiful isn't the mark of a forger. I'd never realized that before. The grass may have been distressed when it was cut, but the danger had passed and the blades flourished in spite of their wounds.

For the first time, I believed I was seeing the world that Erinn wanted to show me, and it inspired me to reach out.

Hey Erinn, what's up?

...

Okay, I could've done better than "What's up."

I'm contesting the order of protection tomorrow, and if it works out, then there's a chance I can get parenting time.

Good 4 U

Wow, I'm really bad at this, I realized.

Let me start over. I'm sorry for using you. I wish I could take it all away. And I want you to know that I care about you, even if I suck at it.

# Quashing the Order

The old bronze seal, positioned just above the judge's podium, had a dull gleam that exuded authority. Judge Mulligan had yet to enter the courtroom, but Eva was there, glaring at me as I kept my gaze fixed on the back wall.

"All rise," the bailiff said, shattering my focus.

Eva and I stood, while the court stenographer remained seated, fingers hovering over the keys, prepared to capture every word we spoke. That was the fastest my heart had ever beat without meth.

Judge Mulligan strode to the podium and told us to be seated. A Dixie cup and a pitcher sat on the desk in front of me. My hand trembled as I poured the water, I only got half of it in the cup.

"We're here to discuss the order of protection filed by the petitioner, Eva Aaronson, against the defendant, Ezekiel Graves." Judge Mulligan said, adjusting her glasses. "Are you both representing yourselves?"

I choked on my water. "Defending myself, yes."

"That's correct, Your Honor," Eva said with a smirk.

Because Eva was the petitioner, she was called to the stand first. I sat listening to her account, my throat swelling shut. She didn't hold back, recounting the fabricated assault on her and Sadie.

Real tears streamed down her face, punctuated by whimpers and trembling.

I clasped my hands under the desk. Blood pulsed through my body. The tranquility I'd discovered at the park was gone. I'd never spent so much time thinking about what my face looked like. Should I show emotion? Is that bad? I tried to look innocent, whatever that meant.

Judge Mulligan's eyes were on me but I couldn't read her expression.

"Mr. Graves," she said as Eva returned to her seat. "Take the stand."

My gaze met the judge's, but my legs froze solid. It wasn't a case. It was a talent show, and I had nothing to offer.

"Mr. Graves," Judge Mulligan repeated. "I need you to take the stand, please."

I dried my hands, stood, and proceeded with my gaze lowered. How was I supposed to look at the judge, bailiff, or stenographer? They'd made up their minds. I could see the disgust in their eyes, and the judge's cold tone solidified my fears when she asked me to describe "my version" of events.

"I went to Eva's house to propose a parenting schedule," I began.

"What happened next?"

"We argued," I said, the words hanging in the tense air. "And I was aggressive with my tone, but I walked away. Eva followed me and grabbed me, then her boyfriend walked out and punched me in the face."

"Why didn't you submit any evidence supporting this?" Judge Mulligan asked.

"Because I don't have any evidence," I admitted. "But there was no assault, so no one has evidence." Then I remembered what Ronald Blake said. "I can show you my phone, where Eva texted me after requesting no contact."

"That doesn't count," Eva scowled.

Judge Mulligan lowered her glasses. "It absolutely counts."

"Eva isn't scared of me," I said, building off the judge's support. "If she were, then she wouldn't be violating her own order."

"Neither of you thought to hire counsel," the judge said, "or provide evidence of your claims."

"My boyfriend saw everything," Eva interjected.

The judge adjusted her position. "You had your time on the stand already," she said. "If your boyfriend was part of your case, then where is he today?"

"I didn't know I—"

"Mr. Graves," Judge Mulligan cut Eva off. "Do you have anything else to say?"

"I can only point out what isn't here. Eva claimed I injured my daughter in the struggle, but there are no medical records. If a grown man assaulted my daughter, I would've rushed her straight to the hospital."

Judge Mulligan shot a derisive glance at Eva as she relieved me from the stand.

I went back to my chair and exhaled.

"Ms. Aaronson." Judge Mulligan addressed Eva critically this time. "In the absence of evidence, I find myself compelled to dismiss this order of protection." The judge shifted her gaze to me. "Mr. Graves, insufficient evidence doesn't make you innocent. I expect there will be no reason for the court to see you again." She hit her gavel on the desk. "I quash this order."

As soon as the gavel fell, Eva plowed through the double doors. If anything was going to help me through the next case, it was her bitterness and my cool head. I paused to drink the water I'd poured and relish my first win for a minute. Then, I thanked the judge for her decision and walked out.

Eva was waiting for me in the hall. "You're not getting shit from me."

"Guess we'll see."

"You're forgetting why I texted you. Ryder and Lez were an item," she said with a smile. "How is she, by the way?"

The floor fell out from under me. Eva knew Lez was a junkie. Which meant she knew what I'd been up to. Leave it to Eva to spoil a good victory and Lez to unwittingly destroy my fucking life.

Before I had time to respond, my phone buzzed.

"This is Zeke," I said, distancing myself from Eva.

"Zeke, Ronald Blake here. I'm not sure if this is good or bad news, but your parenting time request got pushed through. It's two days from now. I've never seen the gears turn this fast. Tell me, have you wrapped up your business with Officer Hallman? You don't want to put your case at risk."

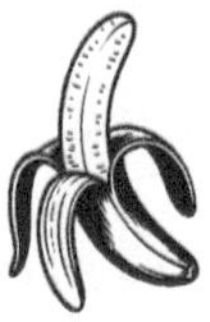

Levi spent the little money he had taking me out to dinner to celebrate. In all the years we'd lived together I'd never sat down at a restaurant with him, not since our mom passed at least. We went to Arriba Mexican Grill.

"You did good today," he said.

I dug my hand into the complimentary tortilla chips, shoving several in my mouth as I responded. "Tomorrow I have to take down a drug-den, and the day after that, I gotta be ready to go back to court."

"Well, try not to choke to death first."

I paused to swallow. "I thought I'd be done with this shit before the next case. For real, bureaucracy gets its ass in gear now, the one time I need it to drag its fucking feet! What am I gonna do?"

Levi put his hand on my shoulder. "You're gonna figure it out."

Before I could protest, a waitress walked up with a plate of sizzling fajitas for me and a bowl of pozole for Levi. Hunger took over, providing a distraction from the fear. I'd deal with Hallman and work out a plan later, first I had to get balls deep in some hatch chiles.

# Take Down

Hallman taped a pinhole microphone to my bare chest, with a thin wire that led to a cellular transmitter hidden in my jean pocket.

"Backslash's bust made sense," he said, snapping his fingers next to the mic to make sure it was broadcasting. "Are you sure we're not wasting time with this Billy guy? Will he lead us to anyone worthwhile?"

"He's gotta get his stuff somewhere," I said. "Look, I've got a hearing for parenting time and legal decision-making tomorrow. I need to get this over with so I can start being a parent."

Hallman responded with a laugh. "This isn't a one and done deal like Backslash. Pay with the marked bills, and we'll see where they lead. If the juice is worth the squeeze, we can talk about timeframes."

"What if there's no juice?"

"Then we try again," Hallman said. "The law doesn't work on your schedule."

"How am I supposed to keep this up?"

Hallman handed me my shirt and hoodie. "You'll figure it out."

I put the hoodie on. Its bulk easily hid the wiring, and no one but Erinn would question a junkie wearing a hoodie, even in the brutal heat.

"Let's get this over with," I said.

Hallman gave me a silent nod and led me out of the station, each of us heading our separate ways to avoid drawing attention.

I was hypervigilant, scanning every mirror as I drove the Dethbox to the deal. Hallman would be circling Billy's neighborhood in his van, available to move in if things went south.

The drive was uneventful, but as I rolled to a stop outside Billy's rundown house, a motorcycle engine revved, sending my heart into my throat. I whipped my head around, but the street was empty.

I climbed out, steadied my hands, and knocked on the door. No one answered, even after I waved at the mounted camera, so I took a note from Lez's playbook and let myself in.

Ash was standing on the other side of the door, fiddling with her fingers. "Hi," she said with a broken smile.

"I need to score some meth from Billy. Is he here?"

"Always," she muttered, then she turned around and trudged through the filth. "I think he's in his room."

I couldn't believe I'd left Ash there. Things were worse than I remembered. The trash was piled high, the stench of decay was almost unbearable, and the crowd of junkies on the floor had multiplied.

Ash led me to the back of the house where the odor intensified. It hit me like a wall when Billy's door opened. Mold had spread across the walls, and buzzing flies filled every corner of the room.

"My friend needs crystal," Ash said, kicking Billy.

Billy stumbled over himself as he tried to stand. Then he pushed aside a laundry pile, revealing a small safe that had been bolted to the floor. He hunched down in front of it like an animal hiding its food.

"Turn around," he said. "Don't look at me."

Me and Ash spun around, our eyes landing on the battered remains of Billy's wall. The dresser by the door looked ready to collapse, and the old tube TV on top flickered with the grainy feed from the front door camera.

Then the roar of a motorcycle shattered the silence. This time, it was right outside. I watched two bikers roll into view.

"Expecting company?" Ash asked.

Billy reached under his mattress and grabbed a gun. "Anytime."

"We have a problem," I said into the mic.

"No shit," Ash replied.

Billy stood with a gun in one hand and a bag of meth in the other. "Give me the cash," he said with the gun pointed at me.

I threw him the marked bills, and he gave me the drugs.

"I think those guys are Desert Vultures," I said, signaling Hallman to move in.

"You know them?" Ash asked.

"No way," I lied, "I can tell by their jackets."

Three-Eyed John came into focus on the TV, and his voice crackled over the speakers. "You took everything," he said, aiming his gun at the camera. "I'm going to take what's mine."

There was a bang, and the screen went blank.

I slammed the bedroom door shut and kicked the dresser over in front of it. Ash and Billy were trying to unstick the window so we could climb out the back, but we were running out of time. As John and his buddy moved through the house, shots rang out, and the sound of screaming junkies filled the air.

Billy left Ash at the window and fired two shots through the bedroom door. Two shots flew back, sending splintered wood across the room.

"You're dead," John shouted through the door.

Sirens cut through the commotion. It was about time.

Billy lined up another shot at the door, and John howled. Four bullets came back. One hit the window, shattering it, two hit the wall, and the third bullet struck Billy's skull, painting the wall with his brains.

I threw Ash out the broken window while John and his buddy pounded the door. The wood cracked, forming lines from one bullet hole to the next, then it collapsed just as I leapt out the window.

Through the tall weeds, I saw Hallman approaching with his gun drawn. He waved us past, and we bolted. I shoved Ash in the Dethbox and burned rubber. There was only one place I could take her.

I burst into Fate's apartment holding Ash. She was in bad shape, and the commotion had gotten to her. She stumbled and fell straight into Zack's lap.

The apartment hadn't changed, and neither had the people. Angel, Sam, and Lez were there, sitting in a circle as always.

"What's Ash doing here?" Fate asked as he came out of his room.

"It's a long story," I answered.

Fate shifted his focus to me instead. "What the fuck are you doing here? I thought you were out."

"I am out," I said, holding up the meth. "But I'm buying Ash back in."

Fate took one look at the size of the bag I was holding and bit his tongue. Zack, on the other hand, could barely contain his excitement. He played with Ash's hair, like nothing had ever happened between them, and it actually felt like something good had come of the deal.

Fate snatched the meth and headed back to his room. "She can stay as long as she doesn't have a needle."

Lez jumped to her feet, lips puckered like she was going to kiss me. I braced myself and pushed her away, but not fast enough. She shotgunned a cloud of thick smoke straight into my mouth.

My heart rate slowed and my muscles softened. It was fucking heroin. After all the hard work I'd put in being sober. How could she? And why would she? My eyelids drooped. It was hitting me hard.

"I need to go," I told her.

"You're going to tell me what's going on," she whispered.

"You could've just asked," I said, feeling the heroin pull me to the ground. "You didn't need to drug me."

There was no way I could drive until my senses were firing, or I'd be nodding off at the wheel. And for some reason, I realized then that this place was never going to let me go, these people would always find a way to drag me back down. I needed to make Fate my next bust and figure out a new plan afterwards.

"Do you really want this?" I asked Lez.

She sat next to me. "I don't know what you mean."

It seemed to me that Lez was like the rest of the crew, a victim of Fate's desire to fuel his own addictions.

"Don't you think that we'd all be better off if Fate were out of the picture?" I asked.

"I knew you were acting fucking sketch."

"You know about Sadie. I'm trying to do the right thing."

"Which is what?" she asked.

I pulled her close, just in case the crew was eavesdropping. "The day after tomorrow, you and the crew need to disappear."

"And where do you want them to go, my place?"

I didn't care where they went. I just wanted them gone. I needed them gone. It's not like I cared much about them personally. They were ancillary characters at best. If this were a story, people would wonder why they were even in it. And I think that's the point. They did nothing but fill the world, and they deserved more than that.

"Look," I said, putting my hands on her shoulder. "You're all better than this. You don't need to sell your body and spend every day doing drugs. Do something with your fucking life."

"So, you are a narc," she said.

"I'm just a guy trying to get his life back. Tomorrow it's Sadie, the day after, liberation."

# Parenting Time

"All rise," the bailiff said. "For the honorable Judge Danielle Mulligan."

Dry mouth had set in overnight, shaking and chills hit first thing that morning. It wasn't much heroin, but it was the first time I'd had it. The courthouse felt like a cage closing in, with fatherhood just beyond its steel bars. All my past mistakes, and all the steps I took to rectify them, had been building towards this one moment.

"We're here to discuss the matter of parenting time and legal decision-making for the minor child, Sadie Aaronson," the judge said. "Both parties are present, and both parties are representing themselves, correct?"

She looked at us for confirmation and received two nods.

"Then be seated," she said. "And welcome back."

Water wasn't helping. My throat was drier than the valley, and my face was heated.

Eva came in hard. "The court should know that Zeke is a meth addict."

I choked on my water.

The judge turned to me and raised her eyebrow. "Anything to add, Mr. Graves?"

"Nothing," I gagged. "Your Honor."

Eva laid out her argument while the voices in my head screamed. For the first time in history, her words held water. Not the bullshit about me never being there, but the comments about the drugs.

I had lost my job, I was using meth, and I had overdosed. Every single detail about the last few months, from my favorite drug to my deepest regrets, was known by Lez, relayed to Ryder, and finally landed with Eva.

Judge Mulligan's gaze was critical when she addressed me. "Ms. Aaronson attests that you never expressed an interest in parenting, and that you only want to see Sadie to lower your child support payments. Most concerningly, she claims you are addicted to methamphetamine. Again, without proof I can only make determinations off of what I'm told."

I took the stand, knocked back from my prior victory, once again at the mercy of the court. I wished I still had my mom's crucifix necklace because I needed a goddamn miracle.

"The only distance that ever existed between me and my daughter is the distance that Eva put between us. The lack of visitation was not due to a lack of effort, but to her unfounded resistance. The truth is, I haven't contacted Eva, and she has no knowledge of my life today."

"Are you saying that there is no truth to her accusations?"

Sweat beaded on my forehead. "I'm not using meth," I answered, and it was true.

I know how it looked. But Sadie would never be subjected to drugs or that lifestyle, no matter what. Hallman and I talked on the phone all morning. Three-Eyed John and the other Desert Vulture were taken out, and Fate was going down next.

"Why do you think that you deserve to be a parent?" Judge Mulligan asked.

"I know the law doesn't see it this way, but I was the best parent I could be. Everything I did was for my daughter. The fact that Eva had complete control of barring me from Sadie's life felt criminal. And if the roles were reversed, it would have been. What I'm trying to say is that when Eva stole my daughter with false allegations, it was like Sadie had been kidnapped."

"I had every right to take her," Eva said.

"That's the problem," I said, turning to her. "You shouldn't have."

"Mr. Graves," Judge Mulligan interjected. "We're not here to discuss your opinion of the law."

"What I mean is I reacted to the situation as it was. For me. My daughter was stolen from me, and I didn't know what to do. I've made my mistakes, but I'm here for my daughter."

"Ms. Aaronson." The judge shifted her gaze. "Sadie is fortunate to have a mother and father who both care for her. Pending the results of today's drug test, I'm granting Mr. Graves court-supervised visitation every other weekend for a period of six months. Unsupervised time will follow this period, and joint legal decision making, assuming there are no setbacks."

"Drug test," I choked.

That should've been the happiest moment of my life. A chance to be a father to Sadie. But Lez shotgunned me heroin. Dread gnawed, twisting my stomach into knots. Not now. Not after everything I'd fought for, and everything I'd risked. I forced a neutral expression on my face, but I'm sure the panic broke through.

"Testing is non-negotiable," Judge Mulligan said. "Show me I made the right decision by being an exemplary parent during visitation and by reporting to TASC for your weekly drug screenings."

"And when does that start again?" I asked.

"Today, as a condition of this ruling, and for the next six months. Sadie will remain in the primary care of her mother. Your biweekly visitation will become parenting time at the end of that period, but there's no compelling reason for me to upend Sadie's current routine."

"Great," I muttered.

The judge smacked her gavel on the bench. "Good luck, Mr. Graves. This is a big step."

# The Support Group

I stepped through the double-door entrance to the church and looked around at the meeting area, then settled in next to the coffee dispenser.

"Are you clean?" I asked the next man who walked up.

He filled his coffee and left. The deadline for the urine test was looming over me, and I was running out of time. I needed someone's piss, and people weren't exactly lining up to drop trow.

I talked to a few guys, but every conversation ended with a refusal. TASC would close in a few hours, and if I didn't pass, it was all over. That's when, out of nowhere, the last person I ever expected to see walked up to the coffee dispenser.

"What the fuck are you doing here?" Backslash asked, sizing me up as she topped off her cup.

Her black dress was gone. She was wearing jeans and a T-shirt. I was proud of her, but what was I supposed to say? I'm just here looking for some piss... Did she know I set her up? She had to know. She must've made a deal with Hallman. I didn't know what to say. My mind was racing, and I rattled out the first question that came to mind.

"How's Damien?"

"Damien's great." She downed her coffee and placed the Styrofoam cup back under the dispenser. "He's always great, the guy's fucking immortal. I, on the other hand, am doing court-ordered rehab because *someone* sold me out."

"What happened?" I asked.

She side-eyed me. “I rolled over on Miguel for leniency.”

We stood there in awkward silence until she asked the question I knew was coming.

“Why did you sell me out?”

“You called the cops on me first,” I said.

Backslash fixed me with a glare. She looked like she was about to explode, but instead she turned and strode out into the parking lot. Then she lit a cigarette, letting the toxic smoke diffuse her.

“Leave me alone,” she said, keeping her back to me.

“I think we both deserve some answers. You know why I sold you out, now tell me why you turned me in.”

“I didn’t,” she said.

“But you apologized for it.”

“I didn’t apologize for turning you in,” she said through a cloud of smoke. “I apologized for how things went down between us. You never should have been wrapped up in that shit.”

Fuck.

If that was true, I was actually the worst person ever.

“Been a while since I smoked,” I said.

Backslash handed me the cigarette with a sigh.

I didn’t plan on becoming a smoker again, but it was a relatively safe way to cope with the bombshell she just dropped. If she wasn’t the girl who snitched to Hallman, then I ruined her life for no reason.

“If it wasn’t you,” I said, handing the cigarette back. “Then who?”

“Who else?” she asked. “The psycho slut.”

“Lez isn’t that bad. She just got wrapped up in the shit like the rest of us.”

Backslash ashed her cigarette. “What really happened to Jenna? I know it was drugs, but I deserve the truth.”

I told Backslash about the heroin sitting out on the counter, that Jenna confused it for coke. And that she died before we could react. There had been a lot of shitty things, but that was the most tragic accident of all.

"That wasn't an accident," Backslash said.

I stole the cigarette for a well-needed puff. "I was there."

Backslash shook her head. "Lez always said that's how you take out a thief."

"Lez isn't responsible for everything that happens. Why would she kill Fate's driver, or call the police on a deal that cost her money?"

Backslash took her cigarette back. "Crazy doesn't need a reason."

Those words stuck in my head.

If there's one thing I understood about Lez, it was her instability. Maybe I'd been looking at her all wrong. What if Fate was just a puppet with a gun, and Lez was pulling the strings? Suddenly, it all clicked into place.

Lez wasn't surprised to see me when I delivered the green guns. She was counting on it. As soon as she learned that she could control me with meth, Jenna's fate was sealed, and the plan went into motion.

"I didn't want to be their driver," I said. "But there was a deal with this guy, Skelton."

"Let me guess," Backslash said. "You got robbed."

"Oh God, Erinn," I realized. "Lez set her up to get raped because she was pissed at us for sleeping together."

"Told you she's a psycho."

Fate wasn't using Lez for sex like I had thought. She was using sex to control Fate, to control both of us.

She tried to get me arrested, and when that didn't work, she shot me up with more meth than I could handle. She would've let me die right then and there if it wasn't for her fuck buddy—the next driver in line.

"Ash warned not to mess with the order... She fucking knew."

"It sounds like everyone warned you about that bitch," Backslash said.

"And I told her that I was going after Fate." I took the cigarette back and smoked it to the filter. "It's all falling apart. I'm about to fail my piss test and fuck up my chance to take down their operation."

Backslash held her hand out. "Give me your ID."

"Why?"

"I have a buddy who looks like you. He's straightedge. The idiots at TASC won't bat an eye. I'll take care of you. You take care of that bitch."

I flicked the cashed cigarette into the street and handed over my license. It was a long shot, but it was my best shot. "Thanks," I said. "Considering how I screwed up your life and all."

Backslash looked me dead in the eye. "Drugs took everything from me, and in a way, you gave me the kick in the ass I needed. I've got a job lined up, and I'll be happy just as soon as you get justice for Jenna."

# The Final Blow

I called Erinn that night. After a couple of rings, it went to voicemail.

"I have a theory about Lez," I said into the receiver. "I've been working as an informant, that's why I didn't leave with you."

A loud crack of thunder startled me, and I looked toward the window.

"Anyway," I said, bringing the phone back to my mouth. "I was going to take down Fate tomorrow, but I tipped off Lez. I don't know what's going to happen. I just need to tell you that I love you."

A second flash of lightning split the sky, and the sudden roar of rainfall hammered the window. My heart pounded as I pulled the blinds aside. A shadowy figure emerged from the downpour, distorted by the sheet of water. I ended the call and immediately dialed Hallman.

"I need your help," I told him. "Someone's at my place."

Levi was asleep, and I couldn't risk dragging him into the shit. Instead of hiding inside the house, I slipped out the front door and onto the patio, straight into Fate's line of sight. He was waiting for me, gun drawn.

"You really thought you could turn me in," he said.

I put my hands above my head. "Let's just talk a minute."

Fate was spun, shaking, and out of breath. I don't think he wanted to shoot me. He'd worn his pistol plenty of times but it was always an idle threat. Lez was the one who did the dirty work.

"You can walk away," I offered. "You don't want this."

Fate's hand trembled. "Shut the fuck up."

One slip, that's all it would take. If his finger so much as twitched, or his grip tightened, everything would be over. I lowered my hands and inched closer, trusting that Fate hadn't come of his own volition.

"Lez sent you, right? You don't have to do this."

He cocked the gun. "You don't know what you're talking about."

Sirens blared in the distance, but I couldn't be sure if it was Hallman, or if help would arrive in time. I lunged at Fate right as a bolt of lightning exploded.

The gunshot that followed was swallowed by the thunder, its force ripping through me before I even knew what had happened. My body hit the ground, and only then did I feel the warmth spreading across my shirt.

I stared at the storm, dazed, as blood pooled around me. The stars were shining overhead, but they were blurry, incomprehensible, stretching ever onward as my eyelids pressed themselves shut.

I could hear Fate pacing frantically, like he couldn't process what had happened.

The sirens were on us. Tires screeched to a stop.

Hallman's commanding voice overtook the storm, "Drop the weapon!"

Fate's gun hit the ground.

Hallman's footsteps approached. The slide of metal sounded. Hallman cuffed Fate and read him his rights.

"She made me do it," Fate said, vindicating me. "Lez, she made me. This whole thing, it's her operation and I'll testify. You just need to keep her away from me, that bitch is fucking nuts."

The next thing I heard was the crackle of a radio.

"Dispatch, Unit 210. I need an ambulance at my location. GSW. Critical."

"Is that it?" I stammered.

"You did good," Hallman said to me. "You're free."

Hallman went back and forth with dispatch, but the words blurred into static, distant and meaningless like the stars overhead. Through the haze, I saw Levi standing over me. His lips moved, but I couldn't hear what he was saying. The sound faded, pain vanished, and the world slipped into darkness.

# Hope

Darkness endured after my awareness returned. The world had been reduced to a void filled with distant, disembodied voices. Panic consumed my thoughts: was this death? I strained to hold on to what little sensation I had left. The voices were the last thread tethering me to existence.

"Thanks for coming," I heard Levi say.

I wanted to speak to him, but nothing worked. It's like my body had disappeared, and I lacked the sensation of having a mouth.

"You said he was awake," a man replied.

"I didn't think the court would send you otherwise, and he needs this."

The next thing I knew, I heard the pound of little footsteps and felt the weight of Sadie's hands grasping my arm.

"Daddy!"

Her excited voice filled the void, and her touch awakened new sensations. A wave of frigid air hit me, contrasting with the heat welling inside. I felt a thin sheet covering me and recognized the sterile smell of the hospital.

A persistent beep grated my nerves, footsteps pounded, and Sadie's worried voice cut through it all, asking what was wrong with Daddy. She must have come with the court-appointed aide.

I imagined speaking the words, "I'll be okay," but I couldn't force them out.

Then, in a sudden eruption, pain returned. The gunshot felt like a cavernous hole, and the anguish seemed to creep further with every moment, catching on my nerve endings and spreading like fire.

"Did he just move?" the man asked.

"Those are involuntary motions," Levi explained.

My brother's somber voice confirmed my worst fears. I might not make it home.

Am I in a coma? Come on, dammit, wake up.

The door squeaked open, and a delicate voice asked to come in. I knew the voice. It belonged to Erinn.

Levi's footsteps moved to greet her. "So you're the girl who was calling Zeke's phone," he said. "I didn't realize he had such good taste."

Erinn took a few noisy steps over the tile. She must have been wearing heels. Her feet clicked with every step. "Hi sweetie," she said. "You must be Sadie. I've heard all about you."

I could visualize Sadie's hand waving frantically.

Then, the bed I was lying on sank. Erinn's hand grazed my face, lighting up more nerve endings, allowing me to feel the external world again.

"I brought you something," she said.

A sudden chill pressed against my chest as Erinn looped her hands around my neck, fastening something cold and familiar—a crucifix. Before I could process the gesture, she took my hand and guided it to her stomach. It was round and taught, just like Eva's had been when she was pregnant.

"This time next year we'll have a family," Erinn said.

I couldn't believe it, Ezekiel Graves, family man. If you asked me a few months ago what the future held, it sure as hell wouldn't have included a drug-induced spiral, or another child, but life never goes the way we plan it.

I didn't know what was coming, but in that moment, surrounded by the people I love, I was happy.

"I know you can't answer me," Erinn continued, whispering so only I could hear her. "But everything is going to be okay. Ash texted me after the crew scattered. Cops raided Fate's apartment, and Lez resisted arrest... It's over, Zeke. We're free to live our lives."

# Also By

Stay up to date with Jonathon's latest updates and releases by following his Amazon Author Page:

# The Author

Jonathon T. Cross is a writer of dark and unsettling fiction, whose stories delve into the depths of decay and the fragility of the human mind.

When not torturing his characters, he can be found in the quiet solitude of the valley, wearing novelty pajama pants. Though his writing tends toward the serious, Cross is known for his playful sense of humor and ability to find light in the darkest corners.

He invites you on a journey into the pages of the unknown, where the boundaries of sanity and reality blur. But heed his warning: once you look too closely, you will never be the same!

www.ingramcontent.com/pod-product-compliance
Lightning Source LLC
Chambersburg PA
CBHW030609310726
48979CB00003B/626

* 9 7 9 8 9 8 8 3 5 2 0 6 8 *